"Get off my back!" Maura snapped

Clayton's face darkened ominously. He stepped around his desk to dominate her with his sheer height. "Whatever I do happens to be for your own good, Maura, so don't get haughty with me."

"Haughty?" she echoed. "I'm not haughty. I'm furious. My inheritance may fall under your jurisdiction, but you don't own me. You're behaving like an arrogant, pompous ass, and I hate you!"

Maura turned to leave, but fingers of steel bit into her arm and spun her around.

"No one, not even you, Maura, will speak to me like that and get away with it!"

Her arms were suddenly imprisoned, and she was jerked up hard against him. All at once she was aware of the warmth of his body, his masculine scent . . . and she had a sudden, crazy notion that he was going to kiss her.

Yvonne Whittal, a born dreamer, started scribbling stories at an early age, but admits she's glad she didn't have to make her living by writing, then. "Otherwise," she says, "I would surely have starved!" After her marriage and the birth of three daughters, she began submitting short stories to publishers. Now she derives great satisfaction from writing full-length books. The characters become part of Yvonne's life in the process, so much so that she almost hates coming to the end of each manuscript and having to say farewell to dear and trusted friends.

Books by Yvonne Whittal

Don't miss any of our special offers. Write to us at the following address for information on our newest releases.

Harlequin Reader Service
901 Fuhrmann Blvd., P.O. Box 1397, Buffalo, NY 14240
Canadian address: P.O. Box 603,
Fort Erie, Ont. L2A 5X3

Bid for Independence
Yvonne Whittal

Harlequin Books

TORONTO • NEW YORK • LONDON
AMSTERDAM • PARIS • SYDNEY • HAMBURG
STOCKHOLM • ATHENS • TOKYO • MILAN

Original hardcover edition published in 1987
by Mills & Boon Limited

ISBN 0-373-02922-5

Harlequin Romance first edition July 1988

CHAPTER ONE

THE wind howled through the trees in the plantation, and whistled around the corners of the stately old house which stood like a fortress on the rise of a hill. There was a brief respite, an almost unearthly stillness, then the wind returned with renewed gusto to pluck at the glass doors leading out on to the terraced garden. Lightning forked across the night sky, and a clap of thunder followed in its wake to shake the foundations of the house beneath Maura Fielding's feet. She was accustomed to these violent summer storms; they passed almost as quickly as they began, and the first heavy drops of rain spattered against the glass doors as she turned away to confront a storm of a different kind which had been brewing in Hilltop House since her arrival that afternoon.

Maura's attractive, finely boned features had adopted a calm and composed appearance, but a tiny nerve pulsed at the corner of her soft mouth. She felt uneasy, and tension had taken an aching grip on every muscle in her small, slender body as her questioning grey eyes encountered the intent appraisal of the man whose austere presence dominated the atmosphere in the room almost to the exclusion of the elements outside.

'Now that you have satisfied your whim, may we hope to see more of you at home and at the office, Maura?'

Clayton Brauer's deep, gravelly voice held a familiar note of censure, and a wry smile curved Maura's mouth then she seated herself in a chair to face her stepbrother across the wide expanse of the carved mahogany desk in his study. Throughout dinner that evening she had been incapable of shaking off the sensation that a loaded gun was being pointed directly at her head, and now she knew it was about to be fired by the dark-haired, dark-eyed man seated in the leather swivel chair behind the desk.

This was the moment Maura had dreaded most. Five years ago her decision to go to college had culminated in the most furious row. Angela Fielding had intervened to reason with her son on her stepdaughter's behalf, and Clayton, convinced that Maura was acting on a whim, had finally agreed rather grudgingly to let her go. The arguments between Maura and Clayton had not ended there, and she knew that what she had to tell him would most likely erupt in yet another unpleasant confrontation.

'I have spent four years at college studying for my teacher's diploma, and I have no intention of allowing that to go to waste.' Maura's grey glance did not waver from Clayton's as she lifted her head in a gesture of defiance and determination. 'I'm a qualified teacher, and I intend to put into practice what I have been taught.'

'My dear Maura, when are you going to accept the fact that you own fifty per cent of the shares in Fieldco, and that you're a major shareholder in the company whether you like it or not?' His smile was amused and tolerant as if he were addressing a child, and Maura's resentment flared swiftly into an anger which she had difficulty in suppressing when he leaned forward in his chair to rest his elbows on the desk blotter. 'You are a wealthy young woman, and I shall appreciate it if you would take a periodic interest in the way I run the company, but there is absolutely no reason for you to go out and work for a salary which you do not need,' he added dictatorially.

The storm outside had reached its peak, and she had to

raise her voice considerably to make herself heard above the sound of the rain battering against the windows. 'You don't have to remind me of my financial status, and I know I don't have to work for a living, but that's precisely what I want to do,' she argued.

'Don't you think you're taking this independence nonsense a bit too far?' he demanded, a familiar frown creasing his wide brow, and Maura sighed inwardly with the sure knowledge that this discussion was leading directly towards the argument which she had hoped to avoid.

'It's not simply a question of wanting to be independent, Clayton,' Maura protested angrily, but she could barely hear her own voice above the noise of the rain lashing the windows with the force of the wind behind it. 'I have to prove something to myself, and this is the only way I can do it. I want to earn a monthly salary, and I want to provide for myself like other less fortunate people.'

A crack of thunder followed her statement. It was so loud it made the light fittings against the wall jingle, and it electrified the strained atmosphere in the book-lined study as their glances and their wills clashed. Clayton's tanned, hawk-like features were set in rigid lines of disapproval, and his attractively chiselled mouth was tight with an anger which was reflected sharply in his eyes beneath the straight, dark brows. It was odd that her mind should choose that particular moment to recall the laughter, the warmth, and the closeness they had once shared despite the ten-year gap in their ages, and it was sad to think of a time which could never be recaptured. In recent years an inexplicable tension had developed between them, and it had become almost impossible to indulge in a conversation without it terminating in a verbal battle.

'Dammit, Maura!' Clayton's harsh, accusing voice made her start, and it brought her back sharply to the present. 'You're being foolish and obstinate as usual!'

'That's *your* opinion, Clayton, but I'm twenty-two, and you no longer have the right to veto my decisions.'

She had gone too far, she knew it, but it was too late to retract her statement. A nerve leapt in his lean cheek as a sure indication that his unfathomable anger had been raised to an explosive level, but his wide shoulders moved slightly beneath the confining cotton of his expensive white shirt in a visible attempt to leash the temper which, as a child, she had not known he possessed.

'You're a young woman with a considerable fortune to her name, and since I have control of that fortune until you're twenty-five I consider that I still have the right to expect to be told what it is you're planning to do.'

His voice had been laced with that icy, controlled anger, and she could feel that awful chasm widening between them, but that was something she would mourn in private.

'I was lucky enough to get a post at the primary school here in New Ansbach.' Maura spoke with a deliberate calm, but there was a slight tremor in the hand which she raised to brush a heavy strand of corn-gold hair away from her pale face. 'I have also accepted an offer to share a cottage in town with one of the other teachers.'

Clayton's face darkened with outrage. 'We're ten kilometres from town! If you *have* to teach, then what's wrong with living here in your own home and travelling that short distance every day?'

'That would defeat the object of this exercise.' She raised gold-tipped lashes to meet his dark, penetrating glance. 'I'll come home at weekends, though.'

His mouth twisted in a savage, derisive smile. 'How generous of you to consider honouring Mother and me with your presence here at weekends.'

'Your sarcasm is uncalled-for!' she snapped, allowing her anger to surface for the first time, but Clayton shrugged it off and took his time lighting a cigarette.

'Is Mother aware of this decision of yours?'

Smoke jetted from his nostrils, and she felt uncomfortable beneath his narrow-eyed appraisal. 'Yes, she knows,' Maura answered warily.

'Did she approve?'

The storm outside was abating, and Maura wished that the same could be said about the storm which was still raging in Clayton's study as she nodded and whispered, 'She did.'

'That doesn't surprise me!' He drew hard on his cigarette and smiled twistedly as he blew the smoke towards the beamed ceiling. 'Mother has always approved of everything you choose to do, whether it be foolhardy or sensible, and I'm beginning to wonder what else there is that Mother knows which I have yet to discover.'

Maura's hands tightened on the arms of her chair until her knuckles whitened, and her back went rigid with resentment and anger. 'Are you suggesting that we're in the habit of conspiring behind your back?'

'God forbid that I should do that!'

His mockery brought an angry retort to her lips, but she bit it back and rose abruptly to her feet. 'May I go now?'

His dark brows drew together in an angry frown as he pushed back his chair and crushed his newly lit cigarette into the marble ashtray on his desk. 'I'm not your enemy, Maura,' he said, getting to his feet.

'That's partly the problem.' There was a biting gravity in her response as she recalled the many times when his foresight had prevented her from getting into a serious scrape as a child. 'For as long as I can remember you have removed the stumbling blocks from my path before I actually got to them, and I really do appreciate that, but now I have to start taking care of myself.'

An odd expression flitted across Clayton's lean, dark face, but Maura did not stay to question it. She walked out of the study and quickened her pace as she ascended the carpeted stairs to her room. She had taken the first step towards proving to herself that she was adult and sufficiently mature to cope on her own, but she sensed that her stepbrother was not going to make her task an easy one.

Maura entered her bedroom to find her stepmother waiting there for her, and she detected an endearing hint of anxiety in Angela Fielding's questioning glance when she rose from the window-seat to approach Maura. Always elegantly dressed, and with her dark hair swept into a neat roll in the nape of her neck, Angela Fielding had stepped in to take charge of Maura almost from the day of her birth, and Maura could not imagine that she would have loved her own mother more.

'How did Clayton react to your news?'

A sigh escaped Maura, and she felt herself relax for the first time since her arrival earlier that day. 'I think he took it surprisingly well.'

A look of astonishment flashed across Angela Fielding's face, and her dark eyes studied Maura incredulously. 'He didn't object?'

'Oh, yes, he objected, as always.' There was cynicism in the smile that curved Maura's mouth when she lowered herself tiredly onto the foot of the bed. 'He may object as much as he wishes, but there's no way he can stop me from doing what I have chosen to do, and he knows it.'

'My dear, you must forgive Clayton.' Angela Fielding seated herself on the bed beside Maura, and there was a pleading urgency in her eyes and in the firmness of the hand she placed on Maura's arm. 'My son may resemble me to some extent in his appearance, but in every other way he is the image of his father. He is strong and dependable, a tyrant when crossed in something he believes in, and protective to the point of possessiveness about the things and the people he cares for.'

'I know,' Maura sighed unhappily, 'but it's time Clayton allowed me to grow up.'

'I agree,' Angela nodded, her face grave, then she changed the subject. 'We missed you at Christmas.'

'I missed you too, but . . .' Maura bit her lip and looked away. She had chosen to spend the Christmas holidays with her aunt in Durban in order to avoid a prolonged argument with Clayton, but the festive season away from her home and the people she loved had been an emotional sacrifice which she did not wish to repeat in a hurry. 'It was better that way,' she added lamely.

Angela Fielding made no comment. She did not have to, since Maura knew that her stepmother understood the reason for her absence without being told, and Maura loved her all the more for it.

'It's time we went to bed.' Angela smiled affectionately as she broke the companionable silence between them, and she brushed her lips lightly against Maura's cheek before she rose to her feet. 'Goodnight, my dear.'

The familiar fragrance of Angela Fielding's delicate perfume lingered in the room long after she had gone, and it was strangely comforting. The storm had passed, leaving in its wake that intense silence which had made Maura fear as a child that the world had suddenly stopped turning, and that she was the only living creature left on earth. She had sought comfort on those occasions in her father's bed, tucked in safely between him and

Angela, and the sound of their deep breathing had quietened her heartbeats and had lulled her to sleep.

Sleep. Maura took off her clothes, put on her nightdress and, after removing her make-up, got into bed, but she could not sleep. Her thoughts were winging their way into the past, and there was nothing she could do to curb it.

Maura's father and Gunther Brauer had been neighbours for many years, their wattle, gum and pine plantations stretching acre upon acre as far as the eye could see across the hills and valleys of northern Natal. The escalating cost of transporting their lumber had become a crippling factor, and Gunther Brauer, a German settler married to a South African woman of British descent, had finally agreed to join forces with Robert Fielding in the costly erection of a pulp and paper mill in the heart of their plantations. It had been a risky venture at the time, but Fieldco had flourished steadily to become the profitable enterprise it was today. Gunther Brauer had, however, not lived long enough to witness and enjoy the triumph of their success. His life had ended tragically one stormy afternoon when he had walked unsuspectingly into the path of a falling tree, and he had left his wife, Angela, with a ten-year-old son to raise on her own, as well as half shares in a business which, at that time, still rocked precariously on its foundations.

It was at that traumatic time in the lives of the two families that Maura made her entrance into the world. Her mother, Kathryn Fielding, had apparently never been a strong woman. Her frailness and her susceptibility to illnesses had been the constant concern of her husband and the family doctor. There were to be no children, but fate had taken a hand and, despite all their precautionary measures, Kathryn had become pregnant. It had been a difficult pregnancy and a difficult birth, Maura had been told years later, and her mother had lingered on in a semi-conscious world for several months before she had slipped away quietly in her sleep one night.

Maura's birth, and her mother's eventual death, had multiplied Angela Brauer's responsibilities by her own willingness to take Maura into her home and rear her as her own. Robert Fielding had mourned the death of his wife, but during the ensuing years he had seen in Angela Brauer the qualities of a woman who could share his busy life and fill his lonely heart. They had married quietly in New Ansbach when Maura was five and Clayton was fifteen, and there might have followed a period of adjustment for Clayton, but for Maura it had merely meant a solidifying of the only family she had known.

After nine happy years together Robert Fielding had suffered a severe stroke while on an inspection tour of the mill. He had been rushed to the hospital in New Ansbach, but he had died before sunrise the following morning. Maura had been fourteen, and Clayton, at twenty-four, had been forced, prematurely, to take over the reins of Fieldco, but Robert Fielding had trained his stepson well, and Maura's admiration and respect for her stepbrother had escalated. She had always adored Clayton. He had set himself up as her protector and her adviser from the moment they had become united as a family, but Clayton's protectiveness towards her seemed to become something of an obsession with him after her father's untimely death. Maura had not objected at first. She had, in fact, revelled in it, but it was during her last year at school that their relationship began to alter drastically.

Maura had been incapable of finding a reasonable explanation for the change in Clayton, and she had finally concluded that the fault lay with herself. His dictatorial manner had, at last, awakened the rebel in her when she realised that it was *Clayton* who had always stood at the helm of the decisions which *she* ought to have made concerning herself. She did not condemn his behaviour, but instead of gaining confidence in herself, she had begun to feel inadequate and incompetent.

It was this startling discovery which had led to her decision to qualify herself as a teacher. It was what she had always wanted to do, and it had taken a great deal of courage to make her secret ambition a reality. She had to prove to herself that she could stand on her own two feet, and that she could cope without having to turn to Clayton for advice.

Oh, if only she could make him understand what she was trying to do, and if only he would accept it as part of the programme she had mapped out for herself in order to grow up. If only . . .!

Maura paused at the gate of the cottage in New Ansbach to admire the flowering shrubs and fragrant roses, and it felt as if she had at last arrived at a safe harbour. The past two weeks at home with her family had been tantamount to drifting aimlessly in a wildly turbulent sea with the threat of a perpetual storm hovering over her head like a dark, ominous cloud.

Fieldco's chauffer-driven limousine had deposited her at the gate with her suitcases, but Maura had not missed that faintly dubious expression which had flitted across the face of the woman who had come out to meet her, and with whom she was going to share the cottage.

Joan Kilpatrick was a tall, slender, green-eyed blonde, and Maura judged her age around twenty-four when they confronted each other for a moment in speculative silence.

'This isn't anything like your palatial family home, I'm afraid.' Joan's remark was both defensive and apologetic when she picked up one of Maura's heavy suitcases and carried it into the cottage which was inexpensively but tastefully furnished. 'No servants! I hope you won't find it too tiresome to do your share of the cooking and cleaning.'

Maura wanted to laugh, but she hastily stifled the desire and exercised a rigid control on her features. This was not the right moment to deal with Joan Kilpatrick's preconceived notions.

'I shan't mind at all,' Maura murmured reassuringly as she followed Joan down the short passage and into one of the bedrooms which had a window overlooking the small, well kept garden.

'The rooms are small and cramped.' Joan stated the obvious, and once again in that defensive, apologetic manner when she dumped Maura's suitcase on the carpeted floor and straightened.

Maura cast a quick glance about the room with its bright floral curtains, its pine wardrobe and dressing-table, and the single bed which her predecessor had stripped bare of her personal linen. This was luxurious compared to what she had lived in during her four years at college, but she kept this snippet of information to herself when she turned to look at the woman who had been regarding her in speculative silence from the top of her corn-gold head down to her expensive white sandals.

'This room is quite big enough, thank you.'

'The girl I used to share with took a transfer to a school in Durban to be near her boyfriend.'

Maura took a few moments to digest this information, and she finally responded with a polite, 'I imagine you'll miss her.'

'We got on very well together,' Joan enlightened Maura, and a dubious expression flitted across her face once again. 'We had similar backgrounds, you see,' she added with a hint of defiance in her voice as if she wanted to stress the fact that she considered Maura of a different social class.

'I see,' Maura murmured stiffly, not quite sure how she was supposed to negotiate this unexpected hurdle she had encountered.

'Well, I'll leave you to get yourself settled.'

Joan smiled for the first time, but it was a reserved smile and, turning on her heel, she left Maura alone in the bedroom with her suitcases surrounding her like a scantily erected fortress.

'Well, this is what you wanted, Maura,' she told herself humorously as she stepped lightly over the suitcases surrounding her and selected the one in which she had packed her linen. 'You wanted to learn to stand on your own two feet, and it seems as though Joan Kilpatrick is going to be a keen and critical observer.'

Maura made up her bed, a task which she had become quite adept at during her four years at college, and then she methodically went through one suitcase after the other until all her clothes and toiletries were packed away neatly into the wardrobe and the drawers of the dressing-table. It was a stifling afternoon, the cicadas were screaming shrilly in the summer heat, and Maura was perspiring freely when she finally stacked her empty suitcases on top of the wardrobe and went in search of Joan Kilpatrick.

'I've made a pot of tea,' Joan announced when Maura entered the small kitchen with its neat wall units and wooden table which could seat four. 'Would you like a cup?'

'I could do with a strong cup of tea,' Maura admitted, wiping the perspiration off her face with her handkerchief, and she lowered herself tiredly on to a chair while Joan poured an extra cup of tea. They sat facing each other across the table, drinking their tea in silence, and eyeing each other speculatively and somewhat warily until Maura voiced the question which had disturbed her from the moment she had stepped out of Fieldco's limousine earlier that afternoon. 'Why did you agree that I could share this cottage with you if you didn't consider me suitable?'

Joan coloured with guilt and embarrassment as she pushed her empty cup aside and lifted her elbow on to the table to cup her chin in her hand. 'I was curious.'

'Curious about me personally? Or were you curious about how a pampered little rich girl would cope with the daily household chores?' Maura questioned her bluntly.

'Both, I guess,' Joan confessed with a matching bluntness that drew a smile from Maura.

'I like your honesty.'

'I like the natural colour of your hair.' Joan responded promptly with an unexpected compliment. 'Mine has to come out of a bottle if I want to look anywhere near presentable.'

Maura could no longer suppress that bubble of amusement which had been growing steadily inside her. It cascaded from her lips in a burst of tinkling, infectious laughter, and Joan's smile widened into a helpless giggle. The ice was broken between them as they shook hands across the table, but Maura suspected that she would still be on trial until she had proved herself as capable, at least, as her predecessor.

'Are you nervous about tomorrow?' Joan questioned Maura when their laughter had subsided.

'A little,' Maura admitted, her expression sobering when she became aware of that fluttering in her stomach at the mere mention of what lay ahead of her.

'The Principal is a bit of a stick-in-the-mud at times, but he's flexible, and he nearly always listens to reason. I can't tell you much about the rest of the staff, but you'll find them all quite pleasant once you get to know them.' Joan lapsed into silence, but her glance was intensely curious when it rested on Maura's attractive, finely sculptured features. 'Would you mind very much if I asked you a rather impertinent question?'

Maura stiffened automatically. She detected it when people wanted to pry into her personal life, but she liked Joan's honesty, and she knew that, if they were to live together in harmony, she would have to reciprocate it.

'I don't mind at all,' Maura replied warily and not quite truthfully. 'What do you want to know?'

'What made you decide to live in town when you could have languished in comfort in your own home?'

Maura's taut body relaxed slightly. She could understand and accept Joan Kilpatrick's curiosity, and it was perhaps only fair that she should tell her the truth. 'I've opted for independence rather than comfort,' she answered cryptically.

Joan looked surprised, but there was also a hint of approval in her green glance. 'I hope you'll forgive me if I quote the local gossips on this, but there is talk of a possible rift between you and your stepbrother, and they are saying that your decision to move into town was disapproved of and accomplished without the blessing of your family.'

Maura sighed inwardly as she leaned back in her chair, and a wry smile curved her mouth. The many and varied speculations of undiscovered origin which so often circulated amongst the locals had always amazed and amused her, but in this instance it irritated her.

'My stepmother has always been very supportive, and I can assure you that I am here in New Ansbach with her blessings, but Clayton is . . .' Maura paused for a moment to consider and to choose her words with care.

'Clayton is mainly concerned about my well-being, and he is inclined to be over-protective. It is because of this that we tend to disagree on certain issues, but it isn't true that there is a rift between us.'

Maura gravely pondered the truthfulness of that last statement she had made. Was there a rift between Clayton and herself? No! Their love for each other had not dwindled, not from her side anyway, but a strange and uneasy situation had developed between them which seemed to lead to a constant clash of wills between them. Clayton took his responsibilities much too seriously where she was concerned, but it would pass. It *had* to pass!

'He's a handsome devil, isn't he?

Joan Kilpatrick's unexpected remark was followed almost at once by a faintly embarrassed laugh, and a startled second elapsed before Maura realised that she was talking about Clayton.

'I—I suppose he—he is,' Maura replied haltingly while she made a vain attempt to see Clayton as other women might see him. He was her brother, and she had never looked upon him in any other way. 'I've never given Clayton's physical appearance much thought,' she confessed with honesty.

'I can tell you there's not an unmarried woman in New Ansbach who wouldn't give almost everything they possess for a night of love with Clayton Brauer, and it wouldn't surprise me to learn that some of the more brazen ones have succeeded.' Joan had passed on this information with a hint of mockery threaded into her enthusiasm, but Maura's total lack of response made her add incredulously, 'You *do* know, of course, that your stepbrother is considered the sexiest and the most eligible bachelor within a fifty-kilometre radius of New Ansbach?'

Maura digested this with a measure of distaste and something else which she could not define. It was ridiculous of her to be so stupidly ignorant where Clayton was concerned. He was a wealthy man in his own right, and if he was the 'handsome devil' Joan claimed him to be, then it was perhaps only natural that women clamoured for his attentions.

'I doubt if any girl thinks of her brother in the same way other women do.' She tried to explain away her reaction, and something in her manner must have given Joan an indication that it would be safer to end that particular conversation.

'I'll cook the dinner this evening to give you a chance to find your way around the kitchen,' Joan offered with a sly grin, 'but tomorrow night it's your turn. OK?'

'OK,' Maura agreed, getting up to look out of the back door which had stood open to admit a refreshing breeze. The back garden was small and cemented, and that made her wonder about the neat little garden at the entrance to the cottage. 'Do you do the gardening on your own, or do you have someone to take care of it for you?' she asked Joan.

'I potter around in the garden when I have the time for it,' Joan explained while she began to prepare the vegetables. 'Once a week, though, the owner of this cottage sends someone along to mow the lawn and weed the garden.'

'That's a relief!' Maura laughed self-consciously. 'I have to admit that I know very little about gardening, but I have always enjoyed arranging flowers.'

'That's wonderful!' Joan exclaimed delightedly. 'I love to garden, but I make a hash of my flower arrangements.'

Maura did not say anything, but she could not help thinking that here was one way, at least, in which they might complement each other.

That evening, after dinner, they watched TV for a while before bathing and going to bed, but sleep seemed to evade Maura for a long time. She was thinking about Clayton, and she remembered Joan's remark about his eligibility among women. How odd that she had never paused to consider the possibility that he might one day want to marry and have a family of his own. Maura knew him in all his moods, bar the present one, and she had to admit to herself that Clayton would make a wonderful husband and father. He had all the right qualities, and he deserved a woman who would appreciate him. She tried to imagine what kind of woman Clayton would choose as a wife. Would she be a brunette, a redhead, or a blonde? A disquieting sensation stirred to life inside her. She could not understand it, but for some obscure reason it angered her.

Oh, damn! What did it matter!

She rolled over on to her side, thumped her pillow with her clenched fist for good measure, and she was asleep seconds later.

CHAPTER TWO

THE classes did not start until the Wednesday, but Maura had been at the school since the Monday morning, and the experience had not been as awkward as she had feared it might be. She was fresh out of college, but the Principal and the staff had in no way indicated that they considered her a raw probationer. Their welcome had been warm and sincere, and there had been no time to dwell on her nervousness during the discussions which had preceded the actual drawing up of the class rosters for that year. Those two days prior to the opening day had also given Maura the opportunity to acquaint herself not only with the rest of the staff, but also with her forthcoming duties, and as a result she was not qute so jittery on the day when she had to walk into the classroom to confront a sea of unfamiliar young faces.

The children might have been a little wary of her at first, but they soon settled down to the new routine of the first day at school after the long summer holidays. It started out as a *getting-to-know-you* day with a class register which had to be drawn up, and then it was a matter of handing out textbooks and settling down to some serious work.

It was during the thirty-minute recess that morning that a lanky, sandy-haired man with bright blue eyes straightened from his lounging stance at the staff-room window to saunter towards Maura with a leather briefcase in his hand.

'Hello, there, sweet thing.' He smiled engagingly down into her grey eyes, and he must have seen there her silent battle to put a name to his lean, handsome face. 'The name's William Baker, remember?' he nudged her memory. 'But everyone calls me Will.'

'Forgive the lapse,' she smiled apologetically. 'I shall remember next time . . . Will.'

'We shall be exchanging classes almost daily.' He charmingly continued to refresh her memory. 'I shall take yours for mathematics and science, while you will take mine for English and history and, if you should need my assistance, you merely have to call and I'll come running.'

'That's very kind of you.' She turned from him to place her empty teacup on the table beside her. 'I don't somehow anticipate having problems with the children.'

'You never know,' he persisted mockingly. 'Children can be horrible little brats at times.'

'You should know all about that, Will, since you've never quite grown up yourself,' a cutting voice intervened, and they turned to see Joan Kilpatrick helping herself to a second cup of tea.

Heads spun curiously in their direction, and Will Baker's handsome face instantly adopted an injured look which, Maura suspected sympathetically, hid his true feelings. 'Joan, my love,' he berated the blonde theatrically, 'you speak daggers and, as always, each one of them has pierced my heart.'

'It's more likely that they have pierced your over-inflated ego,' Joan quipped, her sarcasm biting, and Will Baker flinched visibly in yet another theatrical display to conceal his feelings.

'I shall retire to lick my wounds in private,' he announced dramatically before he bowed low like a courtier in Maura's direction. 'We shall meet again,

Maura Fielding. It is inevitable.'

Maura hid her amusement behind a straight face as she watched Will Baker walk out of the staff-room, but for some obscure reason she also pitied him. He was, perhaps, a man caught in a trap of his own making, and the key to his freedom persistently evaded him.

'A word of warning, Maura,' Joan intruded on her disturbing thoughts. 'Don't ever take Will Baker seriously. He'll break your heart for the fun of it, and he'll dance on what's left of it for an extra laugh.'

Maura observed Joan in thoughtful silence. There was a crack in the blonde's disapproving mask, and Maura caught a glimpse of something which made her wonder about the relationship between this tall, slender girl and the suave, handsome Will Baker.

'Are you speaking from personal experience?' Maura questioned her with an affected casualness in an attempt to learn the truth.

'Fortunately not!' Joan's denial was sharp, and a cynical smile curved her generous mouth into a near-grimace. 'I saw through him right from the start, and that's probably why we have remained such friendly enemies during the past two years.'

'He *is* rather transparent,' Maura admitted, but not quite for the same reasons as Joan might have listed. 'Thanks for the warning anyway.'

The bell rang loudly in the corridor, signifying the end of the recess, and they picked up their briefcases to troop out of the staff-room with the rest of the teachers.

'Back to the grindstone,' Joan muttered, grimacing playfully when they had to go their separate ways. 'I'll see you later.'

Maura did not immediately give the incident in the staff-room another thought, but she was forced to recall it later that day when Will Baker stepped into her path during an exchange of classrooms.

'I'm sorry you had to be a party to that barbed conversation between Joan and me,' he apologised with a gravity that somehow did not suit him. 'It must have been confusing and rather unpleasant for you.'

'I found it rather odd,' Maura confessed with honesty, 'but it is really none of my business, is it?'

'I would like to make it your business,' Will Baker insisted strangely, his long-fingered hand on her arm detaining her when she would have walked on. 'I imagine Joan has warned you against the likes of me, since it was she who so fiendishly branded me the Don Juan of New Ansbach.'

Maura glanced down at the sun-browned hand clasping her arm, and she wondered how this casual physical contact would be interpreted by those who were of the same opinion as Joan, but Will Baker released her arm the next instant as if he had tuned into her thoughts.

'Joan did issue a warning of that nature,' Maura admitted, trying not to let him see that she was amused rather than annoyed, 'but I usually prefer to make up my own mind about people.'

'I thank you for that, kind lady.' Will let out a sigh, and a look of relief mingled with the mockery in his blue eyes when he raised his hand to his forehead in a vague imitation of a military salute. 'You have restored my faith in humanity,' he added in that familiar theatrical manner before they parted company.

Maura could not quite make up her mind about Will Baker, and she was in a thoughtful mood when she walked into the history class where the children scrambled to their feet and chorused a sing-song 'Good afternoon, miss.'

'Good afternoon, class. Please be seated,' Maura

instructed, shaking off the disturbing qualities of her encounter with Will, and shifting her mind firmly into the right gear for the history period ahead of her.

That night, when Maura lay awake in bed, she wondered again about Joan and Will Baker, but, as she had told Will, it was none of her business, and she intended to keep it that way. She banished her curious thoughts from her mind, and slammed the door on that part of her memory.

Fieldco's limousine arrived dutifully at three on the Friday afternoon to chauffeur Maura home for the weekend, and the look on Joan's face made Maura decide to buy her own car as soon as she could afford it. She had been tempted to invite Joan home with her, but their relationship was not yet of such a nature that Maura could claim her as a friend, and there was also a deep-seated need in her to smooth out the troubling situation between Clayton and herself before she would dare to introduce a stranger into her home.

Angela's welcome lacked none of the warmth which Maura had always encountered in her stepmother, but the atmosphere became chilly the moment Clayton returned home from the mill that evening. There was no warmth in his eyes when they met hers, and his lips were cool when he kissed her briefly on the cheek. His muttered greeting was directed at the tapestry against the living-room wall rather than at Maura, then he excused himself and went upstairs to shower and change before dinner.

Maura sighed and fingered the diamond pendant which Clayton had given her on her seventeenth birthday. She remembered also how he had fumbled with the catch when he had fastened the chain about her throat, and how he had coloured when she had expressed her delight by flinging her arms about his neck and kissing him.

'I gather Clayton is still angry with me.'

'Not angry, my dear,' her stepmother corrected with a fond smile. 'He is merely stubborn in his disapproval of what you have chosen to do.'

And determined to show it, Maura could have added, but she chose not to. This was something between Clayton and herself, and only they could solve it. 'I shall have to talk to him,' Maura said at length.

'I doubt if talking to him will help at the present moment.'

'I doubt it as well, but I have to try.' There was a catch in her voice when Maura rose agitatedly from her chair in the living-room to join Angela Fielding on the sofa, and her eyes filled with tears when she clasped her stepmother's hands imploringly. 'Mother, I'm not happy about this wall of animosity which has developed between Clayton and me. We always used to be so close, and now . . . now we seem to be sitting on opposite sides of the world.'

Maura's voice was a choked whisper. Her unhappiness over the past years had grown into something which she could no longer cope with. She wished that she could shake it off, that she could learn to live with Clayton's cold, unbending attitude as she had had to learn to accept the finality of her father's death, but she could not bear this senseless and widening chasm between Clayton and herself, and she longed for the closeness they had once shared.

'This is a difficult period of adjustment—for you as well as for Clayton.' Angela Fielding's warm, sympathetic voice intruded on Maura's painful thoughts. 'I'm convinced, though, that what you both need is time to come to terms with the future.'

Time! The word skipped through Maura's mind and triggered a sharp stab of bitterness. How much time did Clayton need to come to terms with the fact that she was no longer a child, and that she was entitled to make the decisions concerning her own future? A wave of hopelessness engulfed Maura, but she refused to surrender to it, and she became all the more determined to confront Clayton as soon as an opportunity arose to speak to him privately.

Clayton was quiet throughout dinner. He barely glanced in Maura's direction unless it was to ask her to pass him something, and Angela Fielding's sympathetic glance might not have been intended as encouragement, but it fired Maura's determination not to let this weekend pass without attempting to regain at least a fraction of the harmony which had once existed between her stepbrother and herself.

Maura could not sleep that night. It was close on midnight, but the heat—and her unhappy thoughts—had kept her awake, and for the past two hours she had been seeking solace as well as an elusive breath of air on the window-seat in her darkened room. The garden was bathed in moonlight, and beyond the high garden wall she could see the tall trees in the plantation etched sharply against the starlit sky. She sighed deeply, and she was wondering if she would ever tire of this view when a shaft of light appeared on the patio beneath her window. The curtains at the glass doors of the study had been drawn aside, and it could only have been Clayton. Why was he still awake at this hour? She leaned forward on the window-seat to see his shadow precede him out on to the stone patio, and she was surprised to see that he was still fully dressed except for the blue jacket he had worn at dinner. She watched him place a cigarette between his lips and, for a fraction of a second, his features were illuminated harshly in the flickering flame of his lighter. He drew hard on his cigarette, making the tip glow bright red in the darkness, and he raised his face towards the star-studded sky to expel the smoke from his lips while he pocketed his lighter. He seldom smoked, and when he did it was usually an indication that he was angry, or disturbed. Maura wondered which it was when she drew back from the window with a fast-beating heart.

Should she risk talking to him now, or should she wait until he was in a calmer frame of mind? If she waited for the latter she might wait for ever, the cynical part of her mind informed her, and she found herself heeding that warning as she reached for her robe and pushed her feet into her soft mules.

Maura was still fastening the belt of her silk robe about her narrow waist when she walked quickly and noiselessly along the darkened passage towards the stairs, and her hand was light on the carved wooden balustrade when she made her way down into the hall where she had difficulty in focusing until her eyes became accustomed to the light.

The study door was closed, but she opened it without knocking and went inside. Clayton was standing out on the patio with his broad, formidable back turned towards her, and he was unaware of her presence until her shadow appeared beside his on the patio. He turned sharply, his dark eyes raking her body from head to foot, and for the first time in her life she felt a twinge of embarrassment at appearing before him in her night attire.

'May I talk to you?' The words came out in a rush while she fought against an unfamiliar shyness, and stepped out on to the patio to position herself partially in shadow.

'Since when do you need permission to talk to me?'

he demanded in a voice which was devoid of warmth, and not in the least encouraging.

Maura swallowed nervously and pushed her trembling hands into the wide pockets of her robe. 'We haven't exactly been sitting on the same side of the fence lately.'

'Who's to blame for that?' He shot the question at her, and she was still trying to formulate a suitable reply when he gestured angrily with the hand that held the cigarette. 'Disregard that,' he instructed harshly, 'and tell me instead what you're doing awake at this hour of the night.'

'I couldn't sleep. It's the heat, and . . .' Her voice trailed off into silence when her throat tightened with a sudden rush of tears, and she lowered her head until her corn-gold hair fell forward across her shoulders to conceal her distress from those dark, probing eyes, but the loud chirping of the crickets in the undergrowth jarred her raw nerves and prompted her to continue. 'Clayton, can't we be friends?' she rushed on imploringly.

'There can never be friendship between brothers and sisters.'

'You're right.' She acknowledged his statement quietly after giving it a moment of sensible thought, and she raised her glance to his when she had regained sufficient control of her quivering features. 'Between brothers and sisters there can never be friendship. There can only be love and respect . . . and understanding.'

His eyes had narrowed to angry slits, and the muscles seemed to jut out along the side of his jaw when he raised his cigarette to his lips and drew hard on it. 'Are you suggesting that I haven't been understanding?'

'I wasn't suggesting anything, but I do wish you would accept the fact that I believe in what I'm doing, and that I'm happy with my choice of profession.' Her breath caught nervously in her throat when he spun away from her to stare out across the moonlit garden. 'Or, doesn't my happiness count?' she felt compelled to ask.

'Your happiness is all I care about,' he said without turning.

His words warmed her, and she stepped from the shadows to place a hand on his arm, willing him mentally and physically to face her. He dropped the remainder of his cigarette on to the stone patio, shaking off her hand as he did so, and he crushed the cigarette beneath the heel of his expensive shoe before he complied with her unspoken wish.

'I believe you, Clayton, but you can't always be there to smooth out the wrinkles for me when they present themselves,' Maura rebuked him without rancour when he stood facing her. 'I have to learn to do that for myself, and I have to learn to do it in my own way, but I would like to know that I have your moral support.'

'I haven't placed any obstacles in your path, have I?'

'No, you haven't, but neither have you approved.' His tall, wide-shouldered frame was motionless, his manner unrelenting, and she had to tilt her head back to look up at him even though they stood more than a pace away from each other. 'I need your approval if I'm to succeed, and . . . please . . . let's call a truce.'

She held out her hand in a significant gesture of appeal, and for one frightening moment she thought he was going to ignore her, then his warm, strong hand clasped hers and raised it to his lips in an uncharacteristic gesture which made her heart skip an uncertain beat.

'You have my approval,' he said, releasing her fingers

and letting his hand fall to his side.

'But?' she prompted anxiously, knowing him so well that she did not doubt there would be a condition attached to his approval, and he promptly confirmed this.

'Will you promise not to be too pig-headed to tell me if, at any time, you discover you've made a mistake?'

'I promise.' She answered him solemnly, and she made no attempt to hide the anxiety which still lurked in her grey glance. 'Do we have a truce?'

'We have,' he agreed, a glimmer of warmth in the smile he bestowed upon her before his features hardened into a mask of anger which she soon discovered was directed at himself. 'I'm stubborn and selfish where you're concerned, Maura, and I admit that I don't find it easy to relinquish the responsibility which became mine when your father died.'

A warm flood of happiness invaded Maura's heart, and her reaction to his statement was spontaneous and as natural as breathing. 'You're a darling brother, and I love you!' she exclaimed softly.

His cheeks felt rough against her palms when she drew his head down to hers to kiss him on the lips, and she flung herself against his hard chest, wrapping her arms about his lean waist and hugging him to her as she had done so often in the past when there had been no friction between them. But this time it was different. Clayton did not return her affectionate embrace, and his arms remained rigidly at his sides for a few seconds before he raised his hands to take a firm grip on her slim shoulders.

'It's time you went to bed,' he announced brusquely, setting her aside and turning from her to light another cigarette.

'What about you?' She stared at his formidable back,

and found herself battling with the sudden and inexplicable feeling that she had done something wrong.

'I have some thinking to do,' he explained without turning. 'Goodnight, Maura.'

She had the distinct feeling that she was being dismissed, and she wondered why, but she did not linger on the patio to delve into the reason for it. She murmured a hasty 'goodnight', and went inside, breaking into a run as she approached the hall and taking the stairs two at a time.

Why had he behaved so strangely? Maura wondered when she reached her bedroom. Had she perhaps embarrassed him by reverting, without thinking, to her childish habit of kissing and embracing him in a moment of stress, or emotional delight? It had not embarrassed him before, so why should it do so now? The answer leapt out at her like a predator leaping towards its prey, and her cheeks flamed when she recalled her behaviour. She was no longer a child; she was a woman. And if the man had been anyone other than Clayton, then her action might have been misconstrued. His dismissal had been his way of reprimanding her without making a verbal issue of the incident, and she ought to thank him for making her grow up just a little bit more that night.

They were six weeks into the first term at school when Maura decided to put down a small deposit on a pale green, slightly battered Volkswagen Beetle, and she signed an agreement which stipulated that she had to pay a certain sum monthly for the next two years. She was proud of her purchase when she drove through the streets of New Ansbach that afternoon, and there was a look of incredulous wonder on Joan's face when she came out of the cottage to meet Maura on her arrival.

'You amaze me!' Joan exclaimed, circling the Volkswagen and examining it critically. 'I want to be physically ill when I think of the things I said to you on that first day when you moved in with me,' she continued with a rueful grimace when they eventually sat facing each other across the small kitchen table with a mug of coffee in front of them. 'You take an obvious delight in cooking the most delightful meals, and you never complain about doing more than your fair share of the chores when necessary. As if that isn't enough proof that I was totally wrong about you, you go out and buy yourself that—that car outside.'

'What's wrong with my Volkswagen?' Maura demanded, wanting to laugh, but pretending to be indignant.

'Nothing,' Joan assured her hastily. 'It compares favourably with my little Datsun, but it does seem a little ridiculous when you take into consideration that you could afford a more luxurious vehicle.'

Maura's desire to laugh faded swiftly. 'I can't afford anything more luxurious on my teacher's pay.'

'You also have a private income——'

'Which I don't intend to touch,' Maura interrupted testily.

'Why *not,* for heaven's sake?'

'I want to support myself on what I earn as a teacher.'

Joan looked incredulous and bewildered when she combed her fingers through her blonde hair and shook her head. 'I'm afraid I still don't understand.'

'I'm indulging in what Clayton now mockingly calls "a game", but to me it's a matter of deadly earnest.' Maura smiled wryly down into the mug which she held cupped between her hands. 'I have to establish my own identity, and I want to prove to myself that I can accomplish that task without the family fortune to cushion me if I fall. I want to exercise my own discretion, and it can only add to my education if I have to pay for whatever errors I may make along the way.'

Joan remained silent for some time, and Maura wondered what she was thinking, but Joan did not make her wait too long before voicing her thoughts.

'I don't know if you're aware of it, but that's the most you've talked about yourself since you moved in here with me, and I think I'm beginning to understand.' Joan leaned back in her chair, rocking it slightly on the back legs, and her gaze was thoughtful when it met Maura's. 'This is a form of rebellion. You are a strong, resourceful woman with a keen, enquiring mind. You also possess a large slice of independence, and one morning you woke up to the fact that your personality was being smothered by the protective love of your family. You knew they meant it well, but something inside you made you lash out against it and, knowing you as I do now, I realise that there could be no half-measures in this crusade for recognition as a person in your own right.'

Maura felt vaguely embarrassed that she could have revealed so much to Joan without actually intending to, but Joan was not a fool. She was a pretty good judge of character, except where Will Baker was concerned, but Maura was beginning to suspect that there was more to their stinging verbal collisions than either one of them was prepared to admit at this stage.

Maura sighed heavily and got up to rinse her mug in the sink. 'I wish Clayton would try to understand and accept what I'm doing.'

'Talking about Clayton . . .' Joan began, letting her chair down with a thump and pushing it back to get up and follow Maura's example. 'He telephoned while you were out, and he asked me to tell you that he would be coming to town this evening to see you. It's a business matter, I believe.'

'Damn!' A frown of annoyance creased Maura's smooth brow. 'I've got stacks of books to mark, and I'm not in the mood for the business Clayton has in mind.'

'He sounds divine on the telephone.'

'I'm sure he does,' Maura agreed drily, ignoring the gleam of mischief in Joan's eyes and changing the subject. 'Come on, let's get dinner started.'

'It isn't your turn to cook for this evening,' Joan protested.

'If I lend a helping hand then we're bound to be finished sooner, and we might both be able to get some work done before Clayton arrives this evening.'

Maura's explanation was logical, but she suspected that it was the prospect of meeting Clayton which excited Joan's imagination, and which finally made her agree to the suggestion that she could use a little assistance in the kitchen. Maura wanted to laugh, but she suppressed it forcibly and offered to prepare the chicken kebabs while Joan saw to everything else.

Clayton arrived shortly after eight that evening, and his dark, immaculately tailored suit and black leather briefcase indicated clearly that the purpose of this visit was business and not social. His response was pleasant when Maura introduced Joan, but there was an aura of impatience emanating from him which escaped neither of the girls.

'I'll switch on the kettle and make us a pot of tea,' Joan offered, and she retreated hastily into the kitchen while Clayton seated himself in the biggest and most comfortable chair in their small lounge.

'I have here certain documents which need your attention and your signature,' Clayton announced without preamble, opening his briefcase and producing a wad of typed sheets.

Knowing Maura's aversion to the perusal of lengthy legal documents, he proceeded to give her a brief resumé of their contents, and Maura listened intently while he explained the urgent need for expansions to the mill if they were to acquire contracts from farther afield.

Maura's mind wandered briefly. Robert Fielding would have been proud of Clayton if he could have seen him now, and he would have applauded his stepson's ingenuity in seeking a larger market.

She became aware suddenly that Clayton was looking at her rather strangely, and she realised that she must have missed the last fragment of what he had said.

'I'm sorry,' she apologised, blushing guiltily. 'You were saying?'

'I asked if you would sign these documents so that we may go ahead with the plans for the expansion,' he enlightened her with his dark brows drawn together in an angry frown. 'Dammit, Maura! I doubt if you heard a word I said!'

'I heard everything except the last bit,' she assured him indignantly. 'I was thinking about my father, and how proud he would have been if he could have witnessed this expansion you envisage.' She smiled at the look of surprise that flashed across his lean face, and held out her hand. 'I'll sign those documents now.'

The wad of legal papers exchanged hands and, taking the pen he offered to her, Maura flipped through the typed sheets, and attached her signature in the appropriate places.

Joan returned to the lounge carrying a tray on which she had set out their best china cups and, without speaking, she poured their tea while Maura completed her task. An ashtray was placed on the table beside

Clayton's chair when he lit a cigarette, and he rose and thanked Joan politely when she passed him his cup of tea and offered him the biscuits they had baked when they had had a free evening earlier that week.

A faint sigh escaped Maura when she had attached her signature to the final document, and the papers were hastily and safely stashed away in Clayton's briefcase while she helped herself to a cup of tea and a biscuit.

Joan was suddenly in a talkative, enquiring mood now that the business matters had been dealt with, and she was obviously fired with a determination to make the most of this meeting with Clayton. Maura listened and observed them in silence, and she learned something about her stepbrother which she had never known, or cared about, before. He was not an ingoramus where women were concerned. He parried Joan's slightly flirtatious behaviour with aplomb, neither encouraging nor rejecting her, and Maura suspected that her friend was so enraptured that she might have kissed Clayton's feet if he had asked her to when he rose to leave half an hour later.

Joan cleared away their teacups while Maura accompanied Clayton out to where he had parked his sleek white Jaguar. Her newly acquired Volkswagen Beetle was clearly visible where she had left it in the driveway, and he paused abruptly in his stride to stare at it.

'What the devil is this?' he demanded, approaching the vehicle and bending down to examine the dent in the right front bumper.

'They tell me it's a car,' Maura quipped back, instantly on the defensive. 'It has four wheels and an engine, and I'm told it runs on fuel.'

'Don't try to be clever with me, Maura!' he warned darkly, straightening and pointing disparagingly. 'Does this contraption belong to you?'

Her chin rose defiantly, and her eyes sparked with anger in the street-light. 'Yes, it does.'

Clayton let out a savage expletive which he had never used in her presence before, and she took a hasty pace away from him as an anticipated measure of self-preservation when the vibrations of his anger began to envelop her.

'You can't possibly drive around in this thing!' he protested in a harsh, authoritative voice which made her stiffen with resentment. 'It isn't safe! It's . . . my God, this is a mobile death-trap!'

'It's as safe as any vehicle on the road,' she argued coldly. 'I am quite sure that it will get me where I want to be. Perhaps not at the speed which you're accustomed to, but it will get me there all the same.'

'That's wishful thinking!' he barked contemptuously. 'What on earth possessed you to buy it?'

'I liked it, and the price suited my pocket.'

'Don't be damned ridiculous!' he exploded savagely. 'You can afford something a thousand times better than this contraption on four wheels, and you know it!'

'I know what I *can* and what I *can't* afford, thank you very much,' she replied coldly, finding the subject distasteful, and wishing that he would go rather than prolong this senseless argument.

'Maura, I've said this before, and I'll say it again! You're taking this independence nonsense too far, and I warn you that I shan't tolerate it!'

His eyes glittered dangerously, and he turned on his heel and walked away from her with an abrupt 'Goodnight' before she could retaliate.

She watched him drive away, and she expelled the air slowly from her lungs to ease the tension out of her body before she entered the cottage. *Damn* Clayton for being so stubborn! *Damn him!*

Joan looked up from a pile of schoolbooks when Maura walked into the kitchen, and there was a dreamy look in her eyes. 'That stepbrother of yours is really quite something!'

'He's a pain in the neck!' Maura contradicted her angrily when she seated herself at the table and drew her own pile of books towards her.

'I gather you have had yet another of your famous arguments,' Joan observed mischievously, and Maura stiffened with annoyance.

'Were you listening, by any chance?'

'My dear Maura, one look at your face was sufficient to tell me what went on outside before he left,' Joan explained without taking offence. 'I presume he disapproved of the car you bought for yourself this afternoon?'

'Yes!' Maura snapped at no one in particular.

'Are you going to let it bother you?'

'No, I'm not!'

'But it does.'

Joan had placed a surprisingly gentle finger on the problem, and Maura erupted in a burst of pent-up fury. *'Hell,* Joan, I wish he would stop being so confoundedly bossy, and I wish he would leave me alone to live my life as I see fit.'

Joan's glance mirrored mild amusement when she rested her elbows on the table and laced her fingers together beneath her chin. 'He cares about you, any fool can see that.'

'I know he cares, and that's why I . . .' Something, an odd inflection in Joan's voice perhaps, made Maura glance at her sharply. 'I don't think we're on the same wavelength at the moment.'

'We're not,' Joan replied gravely, and with characteristic honesty. 'I think Clayton's feelings for you go far beyond that of brotherly affection.'

Maura stared at Joan for long, incredulous seconds while she digested her statement, then she burst out laughing. 'Don't be ridiculous!'

'I agree that it sounds ridiculous, but that's the impression I got when I saw the two of you together this evening.'

Maura's laughter evaporated with the swiftness of a stray drop of water which had fallen on the sun-baked African soil, and she was suddenly aware of a sick feeling rising at the pit of her stomach. 'Joan . . . he's my *brother!*'

'He's your *step*brother,' Joan corrected calmly, but a rueful, vaguely apologetic expression flitted across her face the next instant, and she gestured dismissively. 'Look, I may be wrong, so don't get hung up about this.'

'I have no intention of getting hung up about it!' Maura assured her adamantly, and she made no attempt to hide the fact that Joan had angered her. 'It's the most ridiculous thing I've ever heard, and it's not worth a second thought!'

Maura picked up her pen and opened the first book on the pile in front of her, but she stared at the childish handwriting on the page without taking in a word of the essay. What on earth had possessed Joan to make such an absurd statement?

'I've offended you with my stupid observation, and I'm sorry,' Joan murmured apologetically as if she had read Maura's thoughts.

'Forget it!' Maura advised, her anger draining away from her along with everything else, and she got up to switch on the kettle. 'I'll make us a mug of coffee, and then we will have to get stuck into these books, whether we like it or not.'

CHAPTER THREE

THE roster for extra-mural activities had Maura's name down with Will Baker's for tennis and rugby football respectively, and she groaned inwardly at the prospect. She was tired. She had stayed up late most nights, preparing lessons and drawing up papers for the end of term exams, and when she did finally get to bed she was too keyed up to go to sleep immediately. This would have been the first afternoon in weeks that she would have had nothing more to do than prepare her lessons for the following day. She had looked forward to the end of the day when she could go home, but instead she was forced to spend a gruelling couple of hours in the hot sun with the young tennis players who were hoping to win a place in the school teams.

Maura was physically drained when, two hours later, she walked to where she had parked her Volkswagen beneath the shady plane trees. She flung her briefcase on to the passenger seat, and she was about to slump down into the driver's seat when the sound of approaching footsteps made her glance over her shoulder to see Will Baker striding briskly towards her with his sandy hair in disarray and his white shirt clinging to his sweat-dampened skin.

'Do you have a few minutes to spare, Maura?'

'Yes, Will.' She suppressed a tired sigh as she brushed a heavy strand of hair out of her hot face, and she leaned back against her car for support while she looked up at him enquiringly. 'What's on your mind?'

'I need help, and there's no one else I can turn to.' He frowned down at his dusty shoes, and he looked surprisingly awkward for someone who was always so suave and sure of himself. 'It's about Joan.'

'I suspected as much,' she murmured, studying him intently, but she found nothing in his attractive blue eyes to give her a clear indication of his feelings. 'Are you serious about her, Will, or is it merely the fact that you haven't succeeded in making a conquest that attracts you?'

His smile came close to a grimace of pain, and Maura knew that she had struck a sensitive chord, but Will Baker did not appear to be offended.

'I admit that I've played the field, so to speak, with women since my college days, and I'm aware that I've collected something of a reputation along the way, but almost from the moment I met Joan I knew that there could never be any other woman for me.' His brows met in an angry frown, but his anger was clearly directed at himself. 'The problem is, I approached her in the wrong way when we first met, and in some uncanny way she seemed to know exactly what kind of man I was . . . or *used* to be.'

His problem was of his own making, but Maura could not help feeling sorry for him. 'Have you tried to explain this to her?'

'She won't let me get near her, and you're aware of the trend of our conversations in the confines of the school.' He sighed and combed his fingers through his hair in obvious agitation and despair. 'This has been going on for two years, Maura, and I don't mind admitting to you that I'm getting desperate.'

'What do you want me to do, Will?'

'Talk to her, and try to gauge her feelings. If there's no chance at all that she . . .' His voice faded into a croak, and his throat worked as if he were trying to swallow a large, solid object. 'Well, if there's no chance at all,' he continued, 'then I'm thinking of asking for a transfer away from New Ansbach. I've reached the end of the line. I can no longer bear being so close to the woman I care for without being able to reach her mind and touch her heart.' The ensuing silence was broken by his unexpected bark of laughter and, for the first time since meeting him, Maura saw a look of embarrassement settle on his handsome features. 'I do appear to have a sense of drama, don't I, but I've never been more serious in my life.'

He *was* serious, Maura did not doubt him for a moment, but she had no way of knowing whether this knowledge would have the desired effect on Joan.

'I'll do my best for you, Will, but I can't promise anything,' she told him gravely, praying that her desire to help this man would not be frowned upon by Joan as unwanted interference.

'Thank you, dear lady.' He looked relieved, and he smiled as he took her hand and raised it gallantly to his lips. 'You shall always have my undying gratitude, whether you succeed on my behalf or not.'

She watched him walk away, and a disquieting thought occurred to her. If she failed, Will's gratitude would be a poor substitute for the loss of that mutual friendship which had developed between Joan and herself.

Maura drove out of the school grounds, her mind proposing and rejecting several openings to the discussion she had promised to have with Joan, but her thoughts were still an indecisive tangle when she arrived at the cottage.

Joan was preparing a refreshing glass of iced orange juice for each of them when the doorbell chimed loudly.

'I'll see who it is,' Maura offered, pushing back her chair and, leaving her sandals on the floor beneath the table where she had eased them off her tired feet, she got up and walked out of the kitchen.

'Good afternoon, ma'am.' The young man on the doorstep smiled broadly when Maura confronted him. A local motor dealer's name was engraved on the pocket of his white shirt, and the papers on his clipboard fluttered in the hot afternoon breeze. 'It's Miss Fielding, isn't it? Miss Maura Fielding?' he added for good measure.

'That's correct,' Maura answered him warily, and the clipboard was thrust at her with a flourish.

'Would you please sign this delivery note, ma'am?'

'Delivery note?' She stared at him blankly, and her glance skidded over the printed document without actually taking anything in.

'Yes, ma'am.' The young man smiled at her with a cheeky tolerance that made her feel like an idiot. 'It's the usual procedure, ma'am.'

Maura's own patience was wearing thin, and her voice was noticeably tinged with anger when she said, 'I know it's the usual procedure, but I never bought . . .'

Her voice faltered into silence when her glance strayed beyond the young man, and became riveted in astonishment to the flashy red Mercedes parked at the gate. It was a 190 E, imported and expensive, and something clicked in her tired mind, arousing a hateful suspicion. She scanned the delivery note with an angry, fast-beating heart until her gaze settled on that familiar signature, and everything was suddenly crystal clear to her. This was Clayton's subtle way of thrusting his will upon her, but this was one occasion when his arrogant and heavy-handed tactics were not going to work.

'I'm not signing this delivery note, and I suggest you

take that car back to where it came from,' she ordered sharply, barely able to conceal her fury as she thrust the clipboard back into the hands of the astonished young man.

'If you don't like the colour, ma'am, we could arrange an exchange with one of our dealers at the coast,' he persisted, not believing that she could refuse to accept delivery of a vehicle such as the one parked at the gate.

'I like the colour, and I like the car,' Maura assured him bitingly, 'but I still don't want it.'

'But, ma'am it's paid for, and——' The young man halted abruptly as if something had warned him that he was stepping on to brittle ground where Maura was concerned. 'Whatever you say, ma'am,' he shrugged, 'but Mr Brauer isn't going to like this.'

'That's too bad, and I intend to tell him so personally,' Maura countered icily, her insides shaking with the extent of her fury, and the salesman shrugged again as he turned away.

'Are you *crazy?*' Joan demanded in an incredulous hiss, making her presence known to Maura when the Mercedes was being driven away. 'That's the most beautiful car I've ever seen!' she added, following Maura into the kitchen.

'Would you be able to afford a car like that on your salary?' Maura demanded pertinently while she bent down to retrieve her sandals under the table.

'No, but——'

'Exactly!' Maura interrupted, and she was beginning to shake with suppressed fury when she slipped her feet into her sandals and straightened. 'Excuse me, Joan, but I'm going to take a drive out to Fieldco,' she announced, snatching her car key off the hook against the wall. 'There's a man there I have to see about a car, but I'll be back in time to prepare dinner.'

'Good luck,' Joan murmured, a hint of anxiety in her eyes when Maura brushed past her, and marched out of the cottage with a thunderous expression on her face.

Maura's tiredness was forgotten while her mind came alive with anger. Her hands were clamped tightly about the steering-wheel, and her foot was heavy on the accelerator, demanding more from her second-hand Volkswagen Beetle than it was accustomed to giving as she left New Ansbach behind her and headed out towards Fieldco. Clayton's interference had to be stopped, and she was in the right mood to tell him exactly what she thought of his arrogant, underhand behaviour.

The pungent and familiar smell of the pulp and paper mill filled her nostrils when she parked her car at the entrance to the three-storied building which housed the offices of the administrative staff. She got out of her car, and there was a fierce determination in every step she took when she strode into the air-conditioned building and took the lift up to the third floor.

Mrs Thompson, Clayton's mild-mannered, meticulous secretary, looked up sharply behind her typewriter when Maura barged unannounced into her office, and if Maura had not been so angry she might have been amused by the older woman's obvious indecision as to whether she ought to smile a welcome, or issue a severe reprimand.

'I want to see my brother,' Maura announced, too angry to indulge in the usual platitudes, and the startled Mrs Thompson finally gravitated mentally towards an apologetic smile from behind the barrier of her typewriter.

'I'm sorry, Miss Fielding, but Mr Brauer is studying the monthly reports, and he asked specifically not to be disturbed.'

'I don't care if he has a dozen potential customers crowding out his office. I want to see him, and I want to see him now!'

Maura's delicate features had become set in a rigid mask of obstinate anger as she headed towards the panelled door, and Mrs Thompson leapt up behind her desk with an agility which Maura would not have credited her with.

'Miss Fielding, I really can't allow you to——' She was too late. Maura had wrenched open the door, and she had entered the office to stride purposefully across the carpeted floor towards the man seated behind the large mahogany desk with his shirt-sleeves rolled up to above his elbows and his collar button and tie loosened to expose his strong, sun-browned throat. 'I'm so sorry, Mr Brauer.' Mrs Thompson stood wringing her hands in nervous agitation. 'I told Miss Fielding that you were not to be disturbed, but she insisted.'

Clayton's hawk-like features had tightened with annoyance and disapproval, but he set aside the report he had been studying, and inclined his dark head briefly. 'There is no need for an apology, Mrs Thompson,' he assured his secretary in a clipped voice, 'and would you please close the door on your way out.'

'Yes, sir.'

'*Now,* Maura,' Clayton began, a stinging rebuke in his voice and a censorious expression in the dark eyes that met hers when the door closed quietly behind his secretary. 'What is the meaning of this intrusion?'

'How dare you!' Maura stormed at him, not caring that her voice was raised and could be overheard, and her knuckles whitened when she gripped the edge of his desk to support her shaking body. 'How *dare* you buy a Mercedes in my name and without my knowledge, or consent?'

'The Mercedes is a far better proposition that that beat-up old Volkswagen you wasted your money on.' Clayton parried her anger with an infuriating calmness that made her blood-pressure rise by several degrees. 'You'll agree with me once you've driven the Mercedes.'

'I doubt it!' she snapped, straightening abruptly and glaring down at Clayton with a gleam of defiance in her grey eyes. 'I came here to tell you that I had the Mercedes returned to the dealer.'

'You did *what?*' Clayton demanded, and she had the satisfaction of seeing his icy-calm composure crack for the first time.

'I don't want the car! I refused to sign the delivery note, and I sent the car back to the dealer,' she repeated, elaborating a little more this time, and Clayton's eyes glittered with an incredulous anger.

'For heaven's sake!' he exploded harshly, his swivel chair swaying precariously and almost toppling over when he rose abruptly to his feet. 'You had no right to do that.'

The atmosphere was rife with antagonism when they faced each other across the wide expanse of Clayton's desk, but this time Maura was not going to concede defeat.

'I have a car, Clayton,' she remonstrated acidly. 'It's a very reliable little car, even if you refuse to acknowledge it, and *you* had no right to interfere in this abominable way.'

'Now, listen to me, Maura——'

'No, *you,* listen to *me,* Clayton!' she forestalled him sharply. 'I have chosen my present life-style for reasons which you stubbornly refuse to accept, but the least you could do is respect my wishes.'

'I don't know what you're trying to prove with your

obstinacy, or whom you're trying to impress, but, whatever the case, you might as well know that I'm going to put a stop to it. And you know that I have the power to do it,' he warned darkly.

'Get off my back, Clayton!' she snapped, her anger making her reckless. 'My inheritance may fall under your direct jurisdiction until I'm twenty-five, but you don't own me, and I'll thank you to remember that.'

Clayton's face hardened. A nerve jumped in his cheek, and there was a tightness about his mouth that predicted something ominous when he stepped round his desk to dominate her with the mere height and breadth of his stature. 'Whatever I do happens to be for your own good, so don't get haughty with me, Maura!'

'Haughty?' she echoed on an angry, high-pitched laugh, and she clenched her hands at the sides of her shaking body until her nails dug into her palms. 'God knows, I'm so furious with you, Clayton, that I could strike you!' she hissed up at him. 'You're behaving like an arrogant, pompous ass, and I hate you!'

She turned towards the door, intending to leave, but she had gone no more than a few paces when fingers of steel snaked about her arm, biting cruelly into the soft flesh as she was spun round to face Clayton, and she caught her lower lip between her teeth to prevent herself from crying out.

'No one, not even you, Maura, will speak to me like that and get away with it!'

His voice was like the distant rumble of thunder, threatening and dangerous, but she was too angry to heed what it implied.

'What do you intend to do to me, Clayton? Thrash me?' she demanded, and she was made to regret her mocking response the next instant.

Both her arms were now imprisoned in his strong

hands, and she was jerked up against his hard body with a force that made her head snap back on her shoulders. His face was inches from her own, his warm breath mingling with hers, and the smouldering fury in his eyes was tempered with something else which she could not define, but it had the power to disarm her.

She was all at once aware of the warmth of his body against her own, and the familiar scent of his masculine cologne. It stirred something inside her which bewildered and confused her, and her mind seemed to spin out of control. She had a sudden, crazy notion that he was going to kiss her, and for one equally crazy, heart-stopping second she actually wanted him to, but he thrust her away from him with a suddenness that made her stumble and clutch at a wall cabinet to regain her balance.

'Get out of here, and don't you dare barge into my office again without an appointment,' he instructed harshly, turning his back on her and stepping calmly round his desk to resume his seat.

The fire of her anger had turned to ashes and, completely disorientated by what had occurred, she turned and fled from his office. The speed at which she passed Mrs Thompson's desk make the older woman glance up at her curiously, but Maura did not stop to talk, and it felt as if she did not draw breath until she got into her old Volkswagen and slammed the door behind her.

Maura's hand was shaking so much that she had difficulty inserting the key into the ignition, and her heart was racing at a pace which almost suffocated her. Her body temperature seemed to fluctuate between hot and cold as she drove away from Fieldco, and she did not need to wonder at the reason for her disturbed state of mind and body. She was ashamed of herself for imagining that Clayton had wanted to kiss her, and she was shocked and horrified at the knowledge that she had actually entertained the unsisterly desire for him to do so.

What on earth had possessed her to feel that way? Clayton knew her so well. He knew what lay behind every inflection in her voice and every expression that flitted across her face. Dear God! He must have known what she was thinking and feeling at that moment, and that would explain why he had thrust her away from him in such a ruthless manner.

Maura groaned inwardly, and her hands tightened convulsively on the steering-wheel when she felt a wave of self-disgust engulf her. She had been tired and angry in the extreme, and it had affected her emotional stability. She was trying to find an excuse for her crazy behaviour, but it did not erase the fact that she had entertained a fleeting desire to feel the touch of Clayton's lips against her own.

She was in a subdued frame of mind when she arrived back at the cottage, but she was determined to shake off that final and most distressing part of her encounter with Clayton.

'You're horribly pale,' Joan remarked when she subjected Maura to a searching glance. 'Do we celebrate your victory, or mourn your defeat?'

'I'm not sure,' Maura replied with a vagueness that stemmed from her own uncertainty. 'We shall have to wait and see.'

Maura busied herself with the dinner preparations, and keeping occupied gave her the opportunity she needed so badly to sort her muddled thoughts into a reasonable order. She could almost laugh at herself again when they sat down to eat an hour later, but she could not forget those startling feelings which had been aroused in her.

It was some hours later that evening when Maura recalled her conversation with Will Baker and the promise she had made him. They had packed their briefcases in preparation for the following day, and they were lingering in the kitchen before going to bed, but Maura still had no idea how she was going to broach the subject.

'You're in a very pensive mood,' Joan remarked when she passed Maura a mug of coffee and resumed her seat at the table.

'I was thinking about Will,' Maura replied truthfully, and she was amazed at how effortlessly the right opportunity had presented itself. 'Why do you dislike him so intensely?'

'I don't dislike him,' Joan protested airily, but a strangely guarded look had entered her eyes, and it encouraged Maura to probe a little deeper.

'Well, you could have fooled me,' she observed with mock gravity. 'You never have a kind word to say to him.'

'Kind words might lead to an invitation, and an invitation might lead me into his bed for a passionate but brief affair.'

'And it's something more than a brief affair you want from Will Baker,' Maura added when she sensed an underlying pain in Joan's disparaging remark.

'That isn't what I said,' Joan protested once again, her brows drawing together in an angry frown.

'I'm sorry,' Maura apologised hastily, 'but that's what you seemed to be implying.'

'I wasn't implying, I was stating a fact!'

Maura was silent for some minutes, her own problems forgotten when she glimpsed an unfamiliar wariness in the green gaze that met hers over the rims of their mugs when they sipped their coffee, and something prompted her to take an even greater risk.

'Are you afraid that you might fall in love with him?' she asked tentatively.

'Don't be silly!' Joan's empty mug went down on to the table with an angry thump, but her cheeks had paled, and there was a visible tremor in her hands when she raised them to cover her face. 'Oh, God!' she moaned in a muffled voice.

'You *are* in love with him,' Maura whispered with incredulous delight, and the truth at last brought understanding. 'That's why you're always so nasty to him. You're keeping him at arm's length because you're afraid that he might detect that crack in your armour if he came too close.'

Joan's attractive features had become rigid with distaste when she lowered her hands. 'I don't intend to have my name attached to his long list of conquests.'

'Have you ever considered the possibility that he might be looking for something more than a frivolous conquest?'

'Men like Will Baker don't change,' Joan replied cynically. 'Constancy and commitment are two words which don't happen to appear in their vocabulary.'

'I think you're wrong about Will,' Maura argued, realising that she would have to exercise extreme caution if she did not want Joan to suspect that Will had solicited her aid. 'Why don't you give him a chance to prove to you how wrong you are?'

Joan eyed her suspiciously. 'Why have you set yourself up as a crusader for Will Baker's cause?'

'I happen to like him,' Maura explained smoothly, 'and I also happen to believe that men like Will eventually reach a stage in their lives when they find they want more from life than a brief affair, but it's women like you who refuse them the opportunity to reach out and grasp that stability they're searching for.'

'What do you mean . . . *women like me?*' Joan demanded, surprised and indignant.

'Women who have the ability to love deeply and sincerely usually shy away from men like Will because they're afraid of being hurt, and that's exactly what you've been doing,' Maura elaborated. 'Give him a chance, Joan.'

'That's easy for you to say,' Joan argued, rising agitatedly to rinse her mug under the tap in the sink, 'but I'm the one who will have to foot the bill when the hurt is dished out.'

Maura sensed her uncertainty and her pain at that moment almost as if it were her own. 'You're hurting already, Joan, and it will hurt much more if you don't do something about making a bid for the man you want.'

'Is that what you would do?' Joan asked, turning slowly to face Maura with that guarded look back in her eyes.

The pressure was on Maura at that moment, and she took a few seconds to consider Joan's query before she answered her truthfully. 'If I really and truly love a man, then I will most certainly not allow him to walk calmly out of my life without attempting to do something about it.'

Joan bit her lip in thoughtful silence, then she laughed self-consciously. 'Lord knows I've become so accustomed to our barbed conversations that I'm afraid I wouldn't know what to say to Will under different circumstances.'

'Let him do the talking at first, and follow on from there,' Maura suggested, and Joan nodded slowly.

'I might just do that. I'm not saying I will, mind you,

but I just might.'

They switched off the lights and went to bed, but it was her own problems Maura was wrestling with that night, and they kept her awake until the early hours of the morning.

She was thinking about the way Clayton had held her in his office that afternoon. She was remembering also the warmth, and the muscled hardness of his male physique against the softer contours of her own body. Her mind replayed that moment when she had thought that he was going to kiss her, and the results were startling. She began to tremble, her body felt hot and clammy, and her pulse-rate quickened to an alarming pace.

She wished that she could forget that embarrassing incident, but she could not ignore the fact that she had wanted Clayton to kiss her, and that, even now, she was wishing that he had.

Maura took advantage of the first free moment she had on the Friday morning to write a short note to Will, and she had sent it along to his classroom with one of the children.

You have a chance, she had written. *Don't blow it. M.*

A half-hour later, in passing, Will had nodded and smiled his thanks. Maura did not intend to get involved beyond this point, but she was intensely curious to know what tactics he would employ on this occasion to breach that initial gap between them, and she found herself observing them closely later that morning when they met in the staff-room for tea during the half-hour recess.

'Good morning, dear lady.' Will's customary greeting was directed at Maura with a smile before he turned to acknowledge the blonde beside her. 'Joan,' he said, cool and abrupt as he always was with her.

'Good morning, Will,' Joan responded with an unusual calm, and Will's eyebrows rose in mock surprise.

'What? No biting sarcasm this morning? Or are you planning to build up a strong reserve this time before you attack?' he demanded.

Maura was shocked at first, but there was logic in what he was doing, and it finally filtered through to her. Joan's suspicion might be aroused if he strayed too swiftly from the well known path which their relationship had followed the past two years, but Joan surprised Maura most of all with her reply to Will's mocking query.

'I think it's time we called a halt to this war between us and discussed a peace treaty.'

Will's eyebrows rose a fraction higher, and he only barely concealed his delight behind that hint of mockery in his blue eyes. 'Are my poor ears deceiving me, or do I detect an invitation somewhere beneath the surface of that declaration?'

'It's an invitation to a discussion.' Joan smiled up at him with a hint of her usual cynicism curving her lovely mouth. 'Would that be asking too much of you?'

He smiled wryly. 'My dear Joan, after two long years of perpetual bickering I wouldn't want to miss the opportunity of indulging in a civil discussion with you.'

Maura felt like an intruder, and she turned away to help herself to the tea and biscuits set out on a table at the other end of the room, leaving Joan and Will to continue their conversation in comparative privacy.

She was packing her suitcase that afternoon, and she was checking to make sure that she had everything she might need for the weekend at home when Joan sauntered into her bedroom for a chat.

'I thought you might like to know that Will is coming to dinner this evening.'

Maura kept her eyes riveted to the contents of her suitcase to hide her surprise and her pleasure. 'You must have a lot to talk about.'

'It appears so,' Joan confessed, 'but I'm not going to build up my hopes too high.'

'Of course not.' Maura agreed with her soberly, but she was smiling inwardly at the knowledge that she was in possession of a gladdening fact which Joan still had to discover for herself. 'Enjoy your evening with Will,' she added, snapping down the fasteners of her suitcase. 'And remember to keep an open mind.'

'I'll try,' Joan promised, her hands fluttering in a strangely nervous gesture, 'but I don't mind admitting that I'm scared silly.'

'You'll cope.' Maura could not suppress a giggle, and she picked up her suitcase and headed for the door before she said or did something which might give Joan an indication that she knew more than she ought to. 'See you Sunday evening,' she called out a few seconds later, waving as she drove away from the cottage.

Maura was equally nervous about having to confront Clayton after what had occurred the previous day in his office, but when she arrived at Hilltop House fifteen minutes later she was relieved to hear that Clayton had gone to Vryheid on business and that he would not be back until the Sunday afternoon.

The weekend slipped by quietly, but the house was not the same without Clayton's bracing personality, and Maura was thoroughly bored with herself by Sunday morning when she put on her new bikini and went downstairs to relax in the sun beside the pool. She oiled her body to protect it against the stinging rays of the sun, and pulled her cloth cap forward so that the peak protected her face when she lay back on the sun-lounger.

Maura could not be sure how long she had lain there. She had dozed off without intending to, but she awoke with a start when she felt someone circling her navel with a lazy finger, and she sat up with a jolt, pushing her cap on to the back of her head as she did so to find Clayton sitting on his haunches beside the sun-lounger with an amused look on his face.

'You were not expected home until this afternoon.' She said the first thing that came into her mind while her startled glance took in the play of muscles beneath the blue T-shirt, and shifted lower to the matching blue swimming-trunks which left his long, muscular legs exposed for her inspection.

'I decided to come home earlier,' he smiled, his appraising glance making her feel uncomfortably naked for the first time in the bikinis she had always had a preference for. 'I wanted to talk to you about something, and now seems to be a good time.'

She swallowed nervously. 'I'll go and change.'

His hand on her thigh stopped her when she would have leapt to her feet, and he seated himself beside her on the lounger. He released her almost at the same time, but he trailed his fingers along her inner thigh as he did so.

'You look beautiful just as you are,' he assured her. Maura could not answer him, and neither could she look at him. She was a mass of trembling sensations, and it made her feel as disorientated as the day when she had thought he was going to kiss her. 'I owe you an apology.'

She looked at him then, and she was not quite sure whether he was serious or joking. There was only one thing she was sure of at that moment. For the first time in her life she was not looking at him as a sister would look at a brother, but as a woman would look at a man, and that feeling of disorientation was heightened by a stab of alien excitement.

What is happening to me? she thought wildly. She snatched up her towel and dabbed at her hot face, but she was also using the towel as a shield behind which she made a frantic attempt to regain her composure before she made an idiot of herself in the presence of this man, who was rapidly becoming *less* of a brother and *more* of a threat to her peace of mind.

CHAPTER FOUR

THE sun was climbing higher in a virtually cloudless sky, and its stinging heat against Maura's body increased her embarrassment at being so scantily attired. Clayton shifted his position slightly to make himself more comfortable on the lounger, and she could feel the roughness of the short, dark hair on his thigh when it brushed against hers.

'I owe you an apology,' he had said, and she had been too bewildered and confused by her own capricious thoughts to formulate a suitable response.

She realised that he was observing her intently when she discarded the towel behind which she had sought refuge, but he waited with surprising patience for her reaction to his statement.

'Do you owe me an apology?' she asked, trying desperately to sound casual while inwardly she was still a mass of quivering nerves, and she deliberately avoided his probing glance when she leaned back on the sun-lounger in an attempt to ease that strange tension out of her body.

'You were quite right to say that I have no right to interfere in you life,' Clayton elaborated with a grimness that made the low, gravelly pitch of his voice sound like a growl. 'I *don't* own you, and I *was* behaving like an arrogant, pompous ass.'

It was a sobering experience to have her own words flung back at her in this unusual manner, and everything else was temporarily forgotten when she felt caught up in a wave of shame.

'I was angry, and I didn't really mean that.'

'Oh, yes, you did, Maura!' He contradicted her with a gleam of mockery in his dark eyes as he tipped up her flushed face and forced her to look at him. 'You meant every word, and don't deny it!'

It was true; she *had* meant every word at the time, but she had not intended it to sound quite so insulting, and she had to tell him so.

'Clayton, I——'

His fingers brushed against her lips, silencing her. 'Do you accept my apology, Maura?'

'Yes, of course I do,' she said with a touch of impatience when she removed his silencing fingers from her lips, and she clasped his sun-browned hand tightly between her own in her determination to speak her mind. 'Clayton, you set yourself up as my guardian angel a long, long time ago, and you're the one I always ran to for protection when I thought I was in trouble, or felt threatened. I shall always love you for that, but it had got to stop, and you have to let me grow up.'

He sat frowning down at her hands which were still clutching his, and she released him self-consciously, but he did not appear to notice.

'I'm afraid I shall always think of you as my little sister, and I doubt if I shall ever rid myself of the desire to protect you, but I shall make the effort, for *your* sake if not for my own,' he said at length, his twisted smile wrenching strangely at her heart, but he rose the next instant and tapped her playfully on the thigh with his fingers. 'What about a swim before lunch?'

Maura declined the invitation, shaking her head and pulling her cloth cap firmly over her face. 'I'd like to laze in the sun a while longer.'

He took off his T-shirt while she observed him unobtrusively from beneath the soft peak of her cap, and she saw the muscles ripple beneath the deeply tanned skin across his broad back. Clayton had a magnificent physique. She had always known it, but she was aware of it now in a different sense which she still could not fathom, and for some obscure reason she could not take her eyes off him when he walked towards the deep end of the pool. He had long legs with muscled thighs and strong calves, and his wide shoulders tapered down to lean hips with a small, firmly rounded bottom.

Clayton turned, preparing to dive into the water, and even at that distance she could see the neat, surgical scar on his right knee. He was lucky to walk without a limp, but the injury he had sustained some years ago on the rugby field had put an end to his days of playing for the local team, and what had initially begun as therapy to strengthen his injured knee had swiftly become a daily routine when Clayton had had the old cellar transformed into a private gym. It was there, among all those weighted contraptions, that he kept his muscle-toned body in shape and worked off the mental stress and strain which accompanied the high-powered position he held at Fieldco.

Maura closed her eyes and thought about her father. During the last few years of his life they had all been deeply concerned by the visible signs that he was cracking under the strain. He had become irritable and unapproachable, refusing to indulge in something which might have taken his mind off his work, and the fatal stroke he had suffered had not come as a complete surprise to them, but it had left them shattered all the same.

An unexpected spray of cold water on her heated body made her gasp and sit up with a jerk to find Clayton standing beside her, a devilish grin on his face, and drops of water sliding down his body to collect in a pool around his feet.

'Clayton, you *beast!*' she cried, hovering somewhere between laughter and annoyance.

'It's time for your swim.'

He whipped off her cloth cap, and scooped her bikini-clad body into his arms, making her shiver when she felt his cold, wet skin against her own.

'Put me down!'

Her scream of protest had no effect on him and, knowing only too well what he intended to do, she pummelled his chest and shoulders with her clenched fists as he carried her towards the pool.

'Clayton, don't you dare!' she warned when he stood poised on the edge.

'I dare.' He grinned at her in that devilish manner, his hard arms tightening about her wriggling body and, holding her firmly, he jumped into the pool.

Maura barely had time to draw breath before her heated body was forced to become acquainted with the shock of being immersed in cold water, and they went down to the bottom of the pool where Clayton released her so that they could kick themselves to the surface.

'Oh, you *are* a beast!' she accused, coughing and spluttering when they surfaced together, and she swept her wet hair out of her face to glare at him while they trod water.

Clayton wiped a hand over his face, but his devilish grin remained intact. His features were suddenly boyish, and his dark hair was plastered to his head and lying in wet strands across his forehead. Maura had seen him like this often enough in her life, but she had never before encountered this strange, warm stirring inside her that made her feel weak in the knees.

This is ridiculous! She spun round angrily in the water

to swim away from Clayton, and also to escape from those unfamiliar feelings he was arousing in her, but Clayton was determined not to allow her to escape. He followed her, his powerful arms cleaving the water to bring him up directly behind her, and his arm locked about her waist when she would have lifted herself out of the crystal-clear water.

Her heart was hammering wildly against her ribs as if she had indulged in an unfamiliar exertion, and she was embarrassingly sure that Clayton could feel it while he held her a prisoner against his body. His chest was a solid wall against her back, and she was startlingly aware of the equally hard thudding of his heart. *Why?* she wondered, adding bewilderment to the many other confusing sensations which she suddenly had to cope with.

'Are you mad at me?' he said, his mouth close to her ear, and the deep, gravelly timbre of his voice made her nerves quiver oddly in response.

'No!' Her voice was cold and abrupt, but she was terrified she might do something to make him aware of the effect he was having on her. 'I want to get out of the water.'

'Sure,' he laughed shortly, his large hands spanning her slim waist and lifting her effortlessly on to the edge so that she sat facing him.

He did not remove his hands immediately, and for several long seconds she found herself looking down into his eyes. She noticed first the wet, spiky lashes, and finally the absence of the laughter which had creased the corners of his eyes moments earlier. It was strangely unnerving. She wanted to look away, but his compelling glance held hers with a probing intensity that made her feel as if he were attempting to strip her naked down to the very core of her soul. A pulse fluttered in her throat, and his mouth tightened in anger as if he had seen it and disapproved.

'It's time we changed for lunch,' he said in an oddly clipped voice, releasing her to lift himself out of the pool, and Maura sat there for a stunned moment, her eyes wide and bewildered as she watched him pick up his T-shirt and walk with long strides to where he had left his towel draped over the back of a chair on the lawn surrounding the pool.

The sun glistened on his damp body, the muscles moving in supple co-ordination beneath his deeply-tanned skin while he dried himself and pulled on his T-shirt, and Maura got to her feet with a choked sigh to walk on unsteady legs towards the opposite end of the pool where her towel lay on the grass beside the sun-lounger.

She felt as if she had been dumped without warning into a deep well of confusion, and the explanation was as elusive as an unmarked trail in the plantation. Her destination was uncertain, but she felt compelled to go on to wherever this trail in her life might lead.

Clayton was quiet at the luncheon table, and so was Maura. She avoided having to look at him as he seemed to avoid looking at her, and if Angela Fielding realised that things were not as they ought to be between her son and her stepdaughter, then she gave no visible indication that she was aware of it. Her conversation was a monologue of information which did not require a response from them other than an occasional nod. She was a member of most of the local charitable organisations, and she erroneously believed that they shared her enthusiasm for the task she was performing, and neither Maura nor Clayton had the heart to dis-illusion her.

Maura did not ask where Clayton was going when he

left the house shortly after lunch. He sped down the driveway in his Jaguar, and he had not returned home late that afternoon when Maura said goodbye to her stepmother and drove back to town.

She was in a disturbed mood when she arrived at the cottage, and Joan eyed her curiously, but she remained silent as if she knew that this was not the right moment to ask questions. Maura unpacked her suitcase, giving herself time to pull herself together. Later they made supper together, talking about everything and nothing, and it was not until much later that evening, when Joan had poured them a cup of tea in the kitchen, that Maura remembered Will's visit the Friday evening.

'How was your unofficial date with Will?' she asked taking a sip of tea and glancing at Joan over the rim of her cup.

'We talked,' Joan replied evasively, amusement lurking in her green eyes and curving her mouth in a faint smile. 'We talked again yesterday, and again over lunch today.'

'And?' Maura prompted, thrusting her own problems aside for the moment.

'We shall have to wait and see what happens, that's all.' Joan shrugged eloquently, her expression sobering when she encountered Maura's questioning glance. 'I love him, Maura, but I'm not going to rush into anything until I'm convinced that Will is sincere.'

Maura nodded. 'That's understandable.'

During the ensuing silence Maura found her thoughts returning to Clayton. What was it that had angered him? Had he perhaps sensed the change in her physical reaction to him? Was that it?

'Tell me about your weekend.' Joan intruded quietly on Maura's troubled and vaguely embarrassing thoughts. 'I have a feeling that you're upset about something.'

Maura felt a stiffness slide into her facial muscles, and she shook her head. 'It's nothing.'

'It can't be nothing when you've been sitting there for the past five minutes stirring your tea for the second time as if you intend to stir a hole through the bottom of the cup.'

'Oh!' Maura lowered her startled gaze to find that Joan had spoken the truth, and she dropped the teaspoon with a clatter into the saucer to raise her fingers to her temples in an unconscious gesture of confusion. 'I think I must be going crazy!'

'It might help if you tell me about it. After all,' Joan added with that gleam an amused smile, 'one good turn deserves another. Wouldn't you say so?'

Maura realised instantly what Joan was referring to, and she could barely conceal her astonishment. 'Will told you that he'd solicited my aid?'

'If anything is to become of our relationship, then there has to be complete honesty between Will and me,' Joan explained, then she brushed the matter aside with a wave of her hand to indicate that she wanted to concentrate on Maura. 'Are you going to tell me what it is that's bothering you?'

'It's Clayton,' Maura began vaguely.

'Don't tell me the two of you have had another argument!'

'No,' Maura whispered, shaking her head and making a desperate attempt to sort things out in her mind. 'No, it wasn't an argument, it—oh, I'm so confused I can't think straight.'

'What happened?' Joan prompted quietly when Maura lapsed into a bewildered silence.

'Nothing happened . . . nothing drastic, that is, but I——' She drew an anguished breath as she raised her troubled glance, and her grey eyes reflected that deep sense of shame she was labouring under. 'Joan, he—he's my brother, and—and suddenly I'm—I'm entertaining the most unsisterly feelings where he's concerned.'

'He's your *step*brother, Maura,' Joan reminded her with a tolerant smile, 'and there's no law that says you can't fall in love with your *step*brother.'

Maura blinked and paled as if she had received a physical blow, and her mind was momentarily too numb to accept or reject Joan's statement. 'Do you think I'm falling in love with him?' she heard herself whispering incredulously.

'Only you can answer that.'

Maura pulled herself together to some extent to search her mind for the answer, but her thoughts were still in a chaotic jumble, and her feelings were in a turmoil dominated by shame.

'Clayton said something this morning,' she began thoughtfully, her mind releasing a fact which might have been intended as a warning. 'He said that he would always think of me as his little sister, and I know that I don't want to think of him as anything other than my brother.'

'It's all very well to reject the thought in your mind, but what does your heart say?'

'I—I don't know, I—I'm not sure.' The words came out haltingly in her confusion. 'Oh, I—I wish I knew what to do!'

'I'm afraid I can't advise you on this matter,' Joan stated ruefully, 'but I *can* tell you that no one is capable of switching their feelings on and off at will. They have to run their natural course, and they will either fade, or grow into something strong and permanent.'

They finished their tea in silence, but Maura's peace

of mind was shattered. She was filled with anxiety and cold dread at the mere thought that Joan might have spoken the truth. Was she in the process of falling in love with Clayton? No, it was impossible! It was *ridiculous!* She loved him as a sister loved her brother, but she was not *in* love with him. Was she?

'God knows, I pray that this is a phase in my life which will pass quickly,' Maura groaned at length, her anxiety etched in every line of her delicate features. 'I don't want to make an idiot of myself where Clayton is concerned and, above all, I don't want to lose his respect.'

'You're in a sticky situation,' Joan acknowledged gravely.

'I know,' Maura sighed unsteadily, 'and I'll have to get myself out of it, or go under.'

They went to bed, but Maura could not sleep. She did not want to think about the possibility that she could be falling in love with Clayton. She would have preferred to remain in ignorance of the truth, but her mind would not let the matter rest until, one way or the other, she was forced to face the reality of the situation.

It was during the early hours of the morning, when exhaustion had made her resistance crumble, that she finally began to admit defeat. Her feelings for him had deepened over the years into something more than the love of a sister for her brother. It had crept up on her so stealthily that she had been totally unaware of the transition until the woman in her had been awakened to the domination of his masculine appeal.

But why? *Why?* Falling in love with Clayton was so senseless . . . and so absolutely hopeless! She knew she had to shut herself away from it, but it swamped every corner of her tired mind, and left her no room to seek a quiet refuge.

I shall always think of you as my little sister.
Clayton's remark leapt unbidden into her mind to mock
her and to intensify her shame.

Maura did not talk to Joan about her feelings for
Clayton. She kept it to herself as if it were a shameful
secret which she could divulge to no one. In truth, she
wanted to be absolutely sure that she had not simply
become over-imaginative and over-emotional in her
longing to recapture the relationship which had once
existed between Clayton and herself, but if she had
prayed that this was so, then she was very quickly
disillusioned.

She was too busy to dwell on her problems during the
last few trying weeks of that school term, but her
weekends at Hilltop House acted as a constant
reminder, and also revealed that her feelings for
Clayton were growing stronger rather than diminishing.
She tried to avoid him, but she did so without much
success, and then again she was miserable when he was
not there. Her conflicting desires were tearing her apart
inside, and it was a painful experience when she finally
accepted the fact that she *was* in love with Clayton.

While Maura was caught up in her own dilemma Joan
and Will drifted into a steady relationship, and Maura
envied them. Oh, if only she had not complicated her
life by falling in love with a man who would always
think of her as his *little sister!*

The children were in an exuberant mood on the last
day at school before the April holiday, but Maura was
not looking forward to spending the next two weeks at
Hilltop House. School closed early that day, and Maura
drove back to the cottage with a feeling of dread in her
heart at the thought of the idle days ahead of her.

'I'm expecting Will to arrive any minute now,' Joan

confided to Maura when they sat down to drink a quick cup of tea in the lounge. 'I'm taking him home with me for the holidays to meet my parents in Pietermaritzburg.'

'This sounds serious,' Maura teased as she drained her cup and placed it on the tray.

'It is, but I'm not sure yet *how* serious.' A slight frown appeared between Joan's arched brows. 'These two weeks at my home will give us both an opportunity to really get to know each other, and then, I guess, we'll take it from there.' Her green, enquiring glance met Maura's. 'What about you and Clayton?' she asked.

'It's a totally hopeless situation.' Maura leaned back in her chair with a sigh. 'Clayton thinks of me as his little sister, and I'm not going to risk the humiliation of being rejected.'

'It shouldn't be too difficult for you to make him see you as a woman.' Joan studied the slender girl in the green and gold cotton frock which accentuated her femininity and her beauty, and a gleam of amusement entered her eyes. 'May I quote you on something you said to me not so long ago? "If I really and truly love a man, then I will most certainly not allow him to walk calmly out of my life without attempting to do something about it". End of quote.' Her glance was challenging. 'What about it, Maura? Would you be able to forgive yourself if you never made a bid for the man you want?'

'What if I fail?' Maura counter-questioned, her voice husky with the extent of her anxiety and nervousness at the mere prospect of making a bid for Clayton's love.

'Oh, come on, Maura!' Joan laughingly brushed aside her query with a disparaging wave of her hand. 'No battle was ever won without the risk of failure, and as a history teacher you ought to know that!'

'In the battles you are referring to both sides had a fair-to-middling idea where to strike in order to gain a possible victory,' Maura protested.

'Am I interrupting something important, ladies?' a male voice demanded from the open doorway, and they looked up to see Will observing them with a comical but curious expression on his lean, handsome face. 'Was one of you two ladies planning to become engaged in a battle with someone?'

'Not at all!' Maura assured him hastily, grateful for the interruption and casting a warning glance in Joan's direction. 'We were merely indulging in a general and unimportant discussion to pass the time.'

'Would you like a cup of tea before we leave?' Joan offered, and Will's smile was warm and appreciative when he lowered his tall frame on to the sofa beside Joan and placed an affectionate arm about her shoulders.

'Yes, I would, thank you,' he accepted, and Maura gestured to Joan to remain seated.

'I'll fetch a clean cup, and then I must be on my way,' she said, feeling suddenly like an unwanted third when she saw the way they looked at each other.

Maura said goodbye soon afterwards and left, but Joan's words echoed repeatedly in her mind during the drive out to Fieldco. *It shouldn't be difficult for you to make him see you as a woman. No battle was ever won without the risk of failure.*

There was just one small problem. Maura smiled cynically to herself as she turned down the window to let the wind whip through her hair. What could she do to make Clayton see her as a woman, and not as his sister? How could she enter into this battle when failure was not merely a risk, but a certainty? Was she being unnecessarily pessimistic? Was she allowing her judgement to be clouded by her fear of rejection?

Would you be able to forgive yourself if you never made a bid for the man you want? Oh, my, but Joan had been clever in throwing her own words back at her, and Maura had to ask herself that question. Would she be able to forgive herself if she never made a bid for the man she wanted?

The answer to that was *no!* She would *never* forgive herself! If she could accept the fact that she had fallen in love with her stepbrother, then Clayton ought to be capable of falling in love with *her*.

'Oh, it's wonderful to have you home for a couple of weeks,' Angela exclaimed when they met in the hall, and her embrace as always was warm and affectionate.

Clayton's welcome was not as enthusiastic as his mother's when he arrived home later that afternoon. His kiss almost missed her cheek, it was so carelessly aimed, and he went upstairs immediately to shower and change. He left the house an hour later, and Maura encountered a stab of disappointment at the knowledge that he would not have dinner with them on her first night home for the holidays.

'It's probably a business dinner,' Angela explained when Maura glanced at her questioningly, 'and I dare say Clayton won't mind if we pour ourselves a glass of his imported sherry before dinner to celebrate the fact that we're going to have you to ourselves for the next two weeks.'

Maura was not so sure that Clayton would want to celebrate the fact that she would be home for two weeks. The cynical side of her decided that his absence that evening was an indication that he considered being away from home preferable to having to spend time in her company.

That's an uncharitable thought! Maura rebuked herself in silence while Angela opened the drinks cabinet and

and poured sherry into two long-stemmed crystal glasses. Just because you're pining for Clayton's company, and feel cheated, it doesn't necessarily mean that he deliberately arranged to be out this evening in order to avoid being with you.

A glass of sherry appered in her line of vision and she looked up with a guilty start as the glass exchanged hands to find Angela observing her strangely. 'I'm so sorry, Mother, did you say something?'

'I was saying that your Aunt Fiona telephoned this afternoon.' Angela was smiling as she seated herself on the comfortable padded sofa beside Maura. 'She was complaining that she hasn't heard from you since you spent the Christmas holidays with her.'

'I've been rather busy,' Maura explained, experiencing yet another stab of guilt.

'I know, dear.' Angela's slender hand patted Maura's arm with understanding. 'You must remember, though, that Fiona Porter is your late father's sister, and that she and her son Gavin are your only living blood relatives. It wouldn't do for you to lose touch with them, and I wouldn't want them to think that we're keeping you away from them.'

'I'll write to her tomorrow,' Maura promised, sipping at her sherry and trying to relax. 'What else did Aunt Fiona have to say?'

'Oh, there was something about the economic climate affecting Gavin's engineering business, but your aunt is nearly always in a dither when business is discussed, and she couldn't tell me much about it.'

Angela studied Maura closely. 'Did Gavin mention anything to you perhaps?'

'He never said a word.'

Maura frowned as her thoughts drifted to her fair-haired cousin. He was an astute businessman, a few years

older than Clayton, and still very much a man who
enjoyed his freedom from the bondage of marriage.
Could there be something seriously wrong, or had her
aunt's statement about the economic climate merely
been an echo of something which was on the lips of
most businessmen today?

She did not have time to dwell on the subject. The
servants announced that dinner was to be served, and
the conversation at the dinner-table concerned the
progress they were making with the expansions to the
mill. Angela's interest in Fieldco stemmed from the days
when she had been forced to step into her husband's
shoes to make and to authorise decisions as an equal
shareholder until her son was of an age when he could
share the burden with her. Clayton had now taken
complete control of the company, but Angela's interest
had not waned. She had a clear head for business, and
an astute mind which she did not hesitate to use when
the necessity arose.

They had coffee in the living-room and talked for
some hours before Angela went upstairs to her room,
and Maura followed her soon afterwards, but for some
obscure reason she lay awake until she heard Clayton's
Jaguar coming up the long driveway.

The first week at home was not quite the ordeal
Maura had expected it to be. She had not realised how
tired she was and, after spending her days lounging in
the sun beside the pool, she had had difficulty in staying
awake after dinner in the evenings. She saw very little of
Clayton during that first week. He would breakfast
early and leave the house before she left her room in the
mornings, and on the few occasions when they did meet
over lunch or dinner he was polite, but strangely distant.
It hurt, but she was damned if she was going to let him
know it. She could still laugh at herself in private, but

her laughter was tainted with bitterness, and an anger directed at herself for loving so unwisely.

Maura was beginning to feel strangely restless at the start of her second week at home, and on the Tuesday evening in particular. Clayton had sent a message to say that he was going to Vryheid directly from work, and that he would not be home until late. Angela had gone up to her room almost directly after dinner, but Maura remained downstairs. She was not sleepy, and she did not relish the thought of lying awake in her darkened room with nothing but her thoughts for company. It was a warm night, and she wandered out on to the patio to sit and dream under the stars. A nightjar sang in a tree close to the house, and a sigh passed Maura's lips. The nightjar would soon fly northwards to a warmer climate, but, come September, it would be back.

She sighed again, and she was lost in thought until the sound of a heavy step behind her made her leap to her feet to find herself confronted by the tall, silent, and somehow menacing figure of a man. He stepped from the shadows of the bougainvillaea trailing along the wooden trellis, the moonlight falling softly on his features, and her heart began to pound with intense relief against her ribcage when she recognised Clayton.

It was late. *Very* late, she realised when she became aware of that slight chill in the air which always accompanied the midnight hour at this time of the year. She had not realised how the time had flown while she had sat there on the patio steps, and she hoped that Clayton would not think that she had been waiting up for him. But did it really matter?

It shouldn't be too difficult for you to make him see you as a woman. No battle was ever won without the risk of failure.

Maura could not imagine why she should have remembered Joan's words at that precise moment, but she was suddenly in the grip of a devilish and daring mood which was totally alien to her nature.

CHAPTER FIVE

THE moonlight could be dangerously deceptive. It seemed to temper the harshness of Clayton's hawk-like features and mould his sensuous mouth into a smile to match the warmth in his eyes, but Maura could not blame it entirely on the moon. She could sense something different about him when they stood facing each other. She could not decide what it was, but it affected her pulse-rate and filled her with a quivering expectancy which encouraged her in her daring purpose.

'I never heard you drive up, and you scared me almost out of my wits,' she confessed, her head thrown back to meet his probing glance when he approached her.

'Why aren't you in bed?' he demanded without the usual note of censure in his pleasantly deep voice.

'I wasn't at all sleepy, and it has been such a beautifully warm night.' The familiar scent of his masculine cologne mingled with the equally familiar aroma of the toasted cigarettes he smoked occasionally, and the assault on her senses sent a tremor racing through her. 'Are you wishing my holiday was at an end so that I could return to New Ansbach?' she asked him with a boldness which did not seem to belong to her.

'What gave you that idea?'

'You didn't look very happy to see me when I arrived a week ago, and you haven't exactly gone out of your way to make me feel that I'm welcome,' she insisted, challenging him to deny it, and he lifted an eyebrow in sardonic amusement.

'Stop behaving lke a petulant child, Maura, and join me for a drink before we go to bed,' he said, turning from her to enter the house.

A petulant child? Her grimace of distaste went unnoticed as she followed him in silence across the well lit hall and down the right-turning passage into his study where he poured a tot of whisky for himself and a glass of sherry for her.

'I'm not, you know,' she contradicted him, gulping down a mouthful of sherry, and it felt as if the intoxicating liquid hit her stomach and her head simultaneously.

'Not what?' He frowned at her, and the ice tinkled against the side of his whisky glass when he raised it to his lips and swallowed down almost half its contents. 'For God's sake, don't speak in riddles at this time of night!'

'I'm not a petulant child,' she explained, walking across the room to draw aside the heavy curtain, and opening one of the glass doors to admit the cool, scented night air.

'A petulant *woman,* then,' he acknowledged mockingly.

'No.' She shook her head and slanted a quick glance at him. He had discarded his jacket and tie, and he was observing her with an odd intensity. 'Just a woman, Clayton,' she added softly.

'Yes . . . a woman,' he agreed, his expression thoughtful, but there was a hint of mockery in the curve of his mouth. 'And you're a very beautiful woman for a man to have as a sister,' he concluded.

Her heart leapt wildly in her breast, and her second mouthful of sherry was swallowed down with as much nervous haste as the first. 'Am I beautiful?'

'Now you're fishing for compliments,' he laughed shortly, draining his glass and placing it on the corner of his desk before he joined her in the alcove of the glass door. 'What's wrong, Maura?' he questioned her.

'What could be wrong?' she laughed, emptying her glass and not quite sure whether it was the sherry she had consumed so quickly or Clayton's nearness which was making her feel so incredibly light-headed.

'I'm asking *you*,' he insisted calmly, and she was unaware that her eyes sparkled mysteriously when she tilted her head to look up at him. 'You have a strange look about you tonight,' he said, 'and I'm not sure how to interpret it.'

'It's full moon,' she teased, allowing him to take her glass from her and dispose of it. 'At the stroke of midnight I'll change into a witch and I'll fly off on my broom,' she added, stepping out on to the patio and raising her face to the starlit sky as she opened her arms in an embracing gesture.

Maura was unaware that the moonlight had added an enchanting halo of silver to her hair, and an alluring, almost translucent sheen to her throat and shoulders, but she did notice that Clayton was staring at her with a slightly bewitched look on his face.

'There will be no flying off at midnight on a broom, or on anything else, young lady,' he instructed humorously as he followed her out on to the patio.

'Anything you say, sir,' she replied in mock subservience, fanning out the wide skirt of her summer frock as she lowered herself into a deep curtsy at his feet and remained there. 'I am your most lowly and obedient servant, sir.'

'Like *hell* you are!' he laughed, placing his hands beneath her armpits and lifting her to her feet with an abruptness that made her sway against him and clutch at his wide shoulders to steady herself. His expression sobered when he looked down into her upturned face, his glance lingering on her parted lips, and she heard him draw a faint, hissing breath. 'Are you flirting with me, by any chance?'

At any other time Maura would have called a halt to this dangerous pursuit she had embarked on, but the sherry had bolstered her courage, and her senses had been alerted to something in Clayton which made her suspect that he was not as indifferent to her nearness as he wanted her to believe.

'I wouldn't know how to flirt if I tried.' Her heart was beating in her throat when she answered him, and her eyes were on his sensuous mouth which was so close to hers that she could feel his warm breath on her lips.

'Don't look at me like that,' he said thickly, releasing her and entering the study.

'Like what?' she asked, feeling a little bewildered and lost without the support of his hands on her body when she followed him inside and watched him light a cigarette.

'Don't look at me as if you want me to kiss you.'

Maura sobered instantly, her cheeks burning, but her boldness did not desert her, and she quickly regained her composure. 'Would that be so terrible?'

'You're my sister, Maura!' he reminded her harshly, drawing hard on his cigarette and blowing the smoke almost savagely through his nostrils as he turned to face her.

'Correction,' she smiled, determined not to let this moment pass when victory seemed within her grasp. 'I'm your *step*sister.'

Clayton gestured angrily. 'It's the same thing.'

'Oh, no, it isn't,' she argued softly, lessening the distance between them, but she had gone no more than two paces when he raised an imperious hand.

'Stop this!' he commanded, the note of savagery in his voice freezing her on the spot, and she could feel the blood drain from her face to leave her pale. 'Stop this at once!'

She had never seen him this angry before, and it actually frightened her. Were her own feelings so intense that she could have imagined something in him which was not there? Had she gone too far too soon? Her courage disintegrating, she turned and fled.

'Maura!' He stopped her before she could reach the door, his touch like fire against her skin when he took her by the shoulders and turned her to face him. His anger had drained from him as swiftly as it had erupted, and his smile was vaguely apologetic. 'You were merely indulging in a silly escapade, weren't you?'

Maura raised her glance to meet the piercing intensity of his dark eyes, and her heart was beating hard in her throat, choking her. 'Why don't you kiss me and find out for yourself,' she challenged him, surprised at her own audacity.

She expected him to be angry, but instead he was shaking with silent laughter, and she wondered if he was aware that he was stroking her bare shoulders in the most arousing manner.

'You're in a crazy mood,' he chuckled.

'Humour me.' She repeated her challenge while the exciting manipulations of his hands rendered her immobile, and she wondered if he could feel the tremors racing through her. 'Or are you scared?' she demanded softly, an unintentional hint of mockery in her voice.

His smile faded abruptly, and she saw his eyes darken into smouldering embers. She felt his hands trembling slightly against her shoulders, and then he took a firm grip on her soft flesh. He drew her towards him until she could almost feel the heat of his body through the cotton of her dress, but then he seemed to hesitate, and she could almost swear that she saw a flash of guilt mingling with the fire in his eyes.

Oh, no! she thought, determination overruling her pride and her fear of rejection. You've come this far, Clayton, and you're not going to back out now!

Her arms slipped about his waist, her hands working their way up across his broad back as she leaned against him invitingly, and it was then that she made the joyous discovery that she had the ability to attract him physically. His body was aroused, his breathing as jerky as her own, and he groaned as his mouth swooped down on her parted lips to claim them for the first time as a lover. It was an experience which excelled her wildest dreams. His hands roamed her body, and his mouth savoured and devoured hers almost as if he needed to satisfy a craving. There was a strange fire in Maura's blood, and it intoxicated her as it raced through her veins. Her nipples hardened with an aching desire when his fingers explored the curve of her breasts through the cotton bodice of her dress, and she pressed herself closer to him, curving her body into his and marvelling at the incredible perfection. She clung helplessly to his shoulders as she surrendered herself to the primitive emotions he was arousing in her, and nothing could have prepared her for what followed. Clayton thrust her away from him with a violence that made her stagger and clutch at the back of a chair for support.

'My God!' he exclaimed hoarsely, his eyes dark pools of anger in a white, grim face, and his forehead glistening with perspiration in the subdued lighting of the study. 'This must never happen again! *Never!* Do you understand me?'

Maura was trembling uncontrollably, and she was con-

vinced that she must look as bewildered as she was
feeling at that moment. 'Clayton, I—I don't——'

'Play your games with someone else in future,' he cut
in harshly, ignoring the silent plea in the hand she had
extended towards him. 'And I suggest that next time
you choose someone your own age.'

'But Clayton, I'——'

'Get out, Maura!' he interrupted her savagely as he
walked towards the cabinet against the wall to pour
himself another whisky. 'Get out and leave me alone!'

Maura stared at him rather foolishly while he drank
his whisky in one angry gulp and poured himself
another as if he intended to drink himself into a stupor.
Her mind was spinning in confused circles, and the
colour had drained from her cheeks to leave her face as
white as Clayton's. *Why?* Why was he doing this to her
. . . and to himself?

The answer evaded her now, and she dared not linger
where she was not wanted. She had to get away. She had
to escape to the privacy of her room, and later, when
she was calmer, she might begin to understand what had
prompted him to reject something which she was
convinced he had wanted as much as she. She turned
abruptly, tears blinding her as she walked out of his
study, and this time he did not prevent her from leaving.

Why? Why did he do it? Maura asked herself that
question over and over again when she was lying awake
in her darkened room. Why, when she could swear that
his feeling had been as strong as her own, had he
rejected her so harshly? Did he find it so impossible to
think of her as a woman, and not as his little sister?

She sighed tiredly, and rolled over to bury her face in
the pillow when she could no longer curb that
humiliating thought which hovered on the perimeter of
her mind. Clayton was a man like any other. He could

be strong, but under extreme provocation he could yield to temptation just as easily as the next man, and she had provoked him mercilessly. Dear God, *yes!* She had behaved abominably, and she was not sure how she was going to face Clayton again, but she knew that she would have to. She owed him an apology, and she could only pray that he would forgive her.

Maura did not sleep very well that night. She was much too disturbed and restless, and she lingered in bed until late the following morning. She hoped that she would have the opportunity to speak to Clayton during the course of the day, but he did not come home for lunch, and she saw him for the first time across the dinner-table that evening. He was cool and distant, but that was hardly surprising after what she had done, and Maura saw Angela shaking her head disapprovingly over her bryani. *They're at it again. They're not speaking to each other because of a silly argument,* Angela must have been thinking, but she did not say anything.

Clayton excused himself from the table after dinner and took his cup of coffee with him into his study. Maura knew what that meant. He would stay there for hours, catching up on the paperwork which he often did not have time for during the day. She also knew the general rule. *Disturb at your own peril!* Well, this was one night when she was going to risk it.

She drank her coffee and left the dining-room with Angela, but they went their separate ways when they entered the hall. Maura's heart was beating nervously against her ribs, and her insides were shaking when she walked down the dimly lit passage towards Clayton's study. She could not have been more aware of the danger within if he had had a red light flashing above the door, but she squared her shoulders and knocked.

'Who is it?'

Maura could hear the anger in Clayton's thundering voice, and she almost lost her nerve, but she sent up a silent prayer as she entered the study to find Clayton glowering at her from across the wide expanse of his desk.

'I'm busy, Maura,' he said, gesturing angrily at the pile of papers in front of him when she closed the door behind her. 'What do you want?'

Maura did not believe that Clayton was unaware of the reason why she had sought him out. He must know that she owed him an apology, and she wondered why he should want to make it as difficult as possible for her. *Why?* Oh, God, she seemed always to be asking *why* these days, but the answers she sought remained stubbornly elusive.

Their glances collided briefly, and it was Maura who looked away, her cheeks reddening at the memory of what had occurred there the night before. 'My behaviour last night was unforgivable, and I'm sorry.'

'The matter is forgotton,' he said with the brusqueness of one stranger to another. 'Anything else?' he demanded, noticeably impatient.

Maura swallowed nervously and shook her head. 'No . . . there is nothing else.'

'Then I suggest you leave so that I may get on with my work,' he said cuttingly, ignoring her as he picked up his pen and started to make notes in the margin of a typed sheet.

Clayton's rudeness and his callous attitude was like a hard, sobering slap in the face. It swept aside her embarrassment and it triggered off her anger.

'Do you know something, Clayton Brauer?' she stormed at him in a fury, her hands clenching at her sides as she stepped right up to his desk, and she glared at him when he looked up condescendingly. 'Your attitude has shown me quite clearly that you don't deserve my apology. *You* enjoyed kissing me last night just as much as *I* wanted you to kiss me! So why should I apologise to you and allow you to treat me like someone who has committed a criminal offence?'

'Shut up!' he instructed furiously, flinging down his pen as he rose abruptly behind his desk, and he circled it in a few long strides to tower over her menacingly. 'Do you want everyone in this house to hear you?'

'What difference does it make if they hear me?' she demanded cynically, her anger giving her the courage she needed. 'Did we do something we have to be ashamed of?'

'Yes, we did!'

Maura went cold inside as she stared up into his shuttered face, and she shook her head incredulously. 'I don't believe what I'm hearing.'

'Maura . . .' Words seemed to fail him momentarily and he gestured exasperatedly as he turned from her and reached across the desk for his gold cigarette-case. He lit a cigarette, and he did not continue speaking until he had blown an angry jet of smoke towards the beamed ceiling. 'We were raised in this house as brother and sister, and brothers and sisters don't kiss each other the way we did last night.'

Maura was beginning to feel equally exasperated when she found herelf confronted by that now familiar barrier which remained as solid as a steel wall between them. 'We're related only by the marriage of your mother to my father.'

'You may look at it whichever way you wish, Maura,' he said with a biting coldness in his deep voice, 'but the fact remains that we have lived like brother and sister, and I don't intend to deviate from that relationship.'

She stared at him open-mouthed when he stepped behind his desk and sat down. She had a ridiculous desire to laugh and cry at the same time, but she forcibly suppressed that feeling of hysteria. It would not solve anything.

'We kissed, that's all, but you're behaving as if you think I'm going to ask you to make love to me next!' she accused indignantly, searching his rigid features for something which was not there, and finally encountering those narrowed and expressionless eyes which were observing her through a screen of smoke.

'That thought did occur to me,' he drawled, his sarcasm biting deep, and inflicting a pain so intense that she nearly cried out with the agony of it.

She stood frozen and speechless, her cheeks flaming for one brief instant before the blood drained from her face to leave it almost as white as the dress she had changed into before dinner that evening. Clayton drew hard on his cigarette and looked away, displeasure etched in every line of his hawk-like features as if he could no longer bear to have her there in the same room with him, and Maura turned without speaking to walk out of his study.

It seemed to take an eternity before she reached the sanctuary of her bedroom, and when she closed the door behind her the tears would not come. They stung her eyes and clutched at her throat, but no more than a dry, strangled sob passed her lips when she sank to her knees in front of her bed.

The last few days at Hilltop House were the most agonising days of Maura's life. There was a wall of silence between Clayton and herself which she made no attempt to penetrate. It hurt too much and too deeply for her to make the effort.

On the last night of Maura's holiday it was her step-mother's endurance which snapped at the dinner-table to make the first dent in that wall of hostility between her son and her stepdaughter.

'This house has been like a morgue these past few days.' Angela sighed in anger and exasperation, her dark glance darting from Clayton to Maura and back. 'Have the two of you argued again?'

Maura put down her knife and fork, and lowered her trembling hands on to her lap as she exchanged a cold, unwilling glance with Clayton. She was tempted to say, 'Will you explain, or shall I?' but she remained stubbornly silent, and it was Clayton who finally answered Angela's query.

'No, Mother, we haven't argued,' he said, his smile derisive. 'Maura and I have had a difference of opinion, and we still haven't reached the stage where we want to agree to disagree.'

The atmosphere was tense around the dinner-table, and Angela impaled them with a disapproving stare. 'May I know the cause of this disagreement?'

Maura's fingers curled nervously into her palms, her nails biting into the soft flesh, and she did not risk glancing at the man who was seated across the table from her.

'It's a personal matter, Mother, and I, for one, don't wish to discuss it,' Clayton stated bluntly, cutting into his sirloin steak as an indication that the subject was closed as far as he was concerned.

'Maura?' Angela prompted determinedly, her dark, questioning glance resting on her stepdaughter.

Maura stiffened in her chair. She felt embarrassed as well as angry while she stared fixedly at the untouched plate of food in front of her, and she prayed that no one would notice her heightened colour. 'It grates me to have to agree with Clayton,' she said coldly, 'but it *is* a personal matter, and I don't want to talk about it.'

Angela leaned back in her chair with a hint of mockery in the smile that curved her mouth, and she raised her arms in a gesture which embraced them both. 'Well, it's nice to know that you agree on something.'

Maura stared down at the food on her plate, and knew that she would be sick if she had to take one bite. She placed her crumpled table napkin on the table beside her plate, and pushed back her chair.

'Please excuse me, I'm not very hungry,' she explained, rising to her feet and fleeing from the dining-room before anyone could stop her.

Her bedroom window stood open to admit the warm, scented night air, and Maura did not switch on the light when she crossed the room to curl up on the window-seat. A nightjar was singing in the syringa tree outside her window, and she sat there listening to it until she could feel some of the tension easing out of her body.

Oh, what a fool she had been! What an *idiot* to think that Clayton could ever return her feelings! She loved him; she had always loved him, but she had not known, until recently, to what extent and, no matter what happened, she knew that she would never again think of him as a brother. It had taken a great deal of soul-searching for her to accept the fact that she had no cause to be ashamed of her feelings, but Clayton was a man of rigid principles. She was his sister, and he would not allow himself to think of her in any other way.

She blamed herself entirely for what had happened between them. She had stepped out of line, and Clayton had put her smartly in her place. She had tempted him, and he had responded like any normal virile man, but, as he had said afterwards, it must *never* happen again. *Never!*

She drew up her legs and crossed her arms over her knees to bury her hot face in them. Tears of shame stung her eyes, but there was also a touch of anger in those tears: anger against the cruelty of fate which had made her fall in love with a man who would always place himself beyond her reach.

The nightjar was singing lustily and unsympathetically when Maura heard her bedroom door being opened quietly, and she did not need to glance in that direction to know that it was Clayton when her soul seemed to reach out at the approach of its mate.

'Maura?'

'Don't put on the light,' she warned in a whisper when she sensed rather than saw his hand going towards the wall switch. 'You'll disturb the nightjar in the tree outside my window.'

The door clicked softly when he closed it behind him, but the carpeted floor silenced his footsteps when he walked towards her and lowered himself on to the window-seat.

They sat without speaking for several enchanted minutes while the nightjar excelled himself as if he was aware that his audience had increased, and Maura's thoughts drifted along a nostalgic path. They had done this before, Clayton and herself, and they had spent many hours together like this during the months from early spring to early autumn. They had been relaxed and comfortable in each other's company then, but they were not relaxed and comfortable now. There was an almost tangible tension between them for which Maura knew she was to blame. A discussion would clear the air between them, but she knew that she would never again be near Clayton like this without being aware of that deep-seated need he had awakened in her, and she knew that she would always remember that brief moment of passion they had shared.

'It must be years since the last time we sat together on this window-seat listening to a nightjar.' Clayton echoed her thoughts partially, his quiet, gravelly voice breaking the silence between them.

'Time passes,' she whispered sadly, feasting her hungry eyes on his shadowy features, and aware of a burning desire in her heart to reach out and trail her fingers along the rigid line of his jaw and strong, sun-browned throat. 'We've grown older . . . and away from each other.'

Clayton seemed to flinch. Or had it been a shadow crossing his face when a branch stirred in the breeze?

'We've grown older, but not away from each other, Maura,' he contradicted her.

'Oh, yes, we have,' she argued without rancour, but rather with sadness and a deep regret. 'You never used to be sarcastic and insulting, but that's what you were the other night when I came to your study to apologise to you.'

'I'm sorry, Maura.' He leaned towards her, the clean male smell of him filling her nostrils and stirring her senses while his fingers trailed fire across her cool cheek. His hand moved through her hair, leaving her scalp tingling when he placed his fingers beneath her chin and tilted her face up to his. 'I had to do something drastic to bring you to your senses. Don't you undertand?'

'It hurt, but I do understand, Clayton,' she assured him, too close to tears to raise her voice above a whisper, 'and I'm ashamed of myself.'

He drew back his hand as if she had stung him. 'You have nothing to be ashamed of.'

'Oh, but I do!' she insisted, watching him reach into his shirt pocket for his cigarette-case, but changing his mind and leaving it there. 'I'd had very little to eat that evening, the sherry went directly to my head, and I—I embarrassed you and—and made you do something you—you didn't really want to do.'

Her confession ended haltingly and trailed off into an awkward silence. Clayton's hand made a second journey to his shirt pocket, and this time it did emerge with his cigarette-case. He lit a cigarette, and his face was harsh and strangely grim in the flickering flame of his lighter. He inhaled deeply, and blew the smoke out of the window to fill the night air with its aroma.

'I don't know if this will be of any consolation to you,' he said at length, his voice falling rough and unfamiliar on her ears. 'but you're a very attractive young woman, and you were right about one thing. I *did* enjoy kissing you, only——'

'I know', she interrupted him hastily, finding the situation too awkward and too painful to allow him to continue. He was trying to make her feel better, but he was, in fact, making her feel much worse. 'I deplore my actions that night, so I would be grateful if you would consider it as no more than a temporary derangement,' she said, injecting a careless note into her voice, 'and don't worry, dear brother, it will never happen again.'

Clayton sat so still in the dappled moonlight that he could have been mistaken for a statue if she had not seen his eyes glittering strangely in the darkness. She also had an absurd feeling that her statement had not particularly pleased him, and she could not imagine why. She had agreed with him that she would never again expect more from him than what one ought to expect from a brother, and that was what he had wanted. Wasn't it?

'I'm glad we had this talk,' he said tersely, leaning forward to kiss her on the cheek. The desire to feel his lips against her own, just once more, was a torment which could have been assuaged with ease if she had turned her head a fraction. Her body went rigid with the effort to remain perfectly still, and the moment passed, but the desire lingered on. 'Goodnight, Maura.'

She sat curled up on the window-seat, and she could not be sure how much time had elapsed since Clayton had left her room. Her body felt stiff when she eventually moved, and the tears had long since dried on her cheeks. The nightjar had also ceased its song to bury its head, perhaps, beneath its wing. Oh, if only she had somewhere to bury her own head, to forget, and never again to remember.

CHAPTER SIX

JOAN glanced anxiously at Maura when they arrived home from school one afternoon. 'Will is taking me out to dinner again this evening, but I hate the thought of leaving you alone at home.'

'Don't be silly, Joan!' Maura laughed when they entered the cottage. 'I can't possibly tag along with you wherever you go, and I'd much rather stay at home. I'll make myself something to eat, and I've brought a pile of essays home which I have to read and mark before I go to bed.'

'That's all you do these days,' Joan complained, her eyes shadowed with concern. 'You work too hard, you eat too little, and I'm beginning to suspect that you lie awake in your darkened room at night instead of sleeping.' Maura avoided her friend's probing glance and turned away, but Joan's hand gripped her arm to prevent her from leaving. 'Look, I know it's none of my business, Maura, but if you ever need someone to talk to, then you know you can trust me.'

A warmth invaded Maura's cold heart and she smiled shakily. Her secret would be safe with Joan, she knew that, but it was still too raw inside her to talk about what had occurred between Clayton and herself.

'Thanks, I'll remember that.' Maura had had to force the words past that restricting lump in her throat, and this time Joan did not detain her when she walked away from you down the short passage to her room.

Maura's heavy briefcase landed with a thud on the

floor when she closed the door behind her, and she leaned against the door for a moment with her eyes closed to hold back the tears. It was ridiculous, but she needed very little provocation these days to find herself on the verge of tears, and she was tired; so *very* tired of pretending that nothing was wrong when her life had become a dark, endless tunnel with no promise of a light ahead. She had to go on, but she had no idea where she was going, and neither did she care.

The days and the weeks had blended one into the other without substance until the only thing of importance to her was to give of her best to the children, and her reward was in their enthusiastic response in the classroom.

Joan was pottering around in the garden later that afternoon, and Maura was washing her hair when the telephone started ringing. It could only be Will, Maura told herself as she rinsed the shampoo out of her hair, but some moments later there was a knock on the bathroom door.

'It's for you, Maura,' Joan called out to her through the door. 'It's a man, and he says he's your cousin.'

'My *cousin?*' Maura echoed in surprise, her attractively arched brows raised above her questioning eyes while she hastily wrapped a small towel around her head and opened the bathroom door to confront Joan. 'Gavin Porter?' she asked, seeking confirmation from the girl who stood peeling off her garden gloves.

'That's the name he gave,' Joan nodded, smiling as she stepped past Maura to wash her hands while Maura almost ran down the passage and into the lounge to take the call.

'Hello, Gavin,' Maura greeted her cousin warily, her mind conjuring up several unpleasant reasons for this unexpected call.

'Maura, my dear, it's so nice to hear your voice again,' Gavin announced smoothly, and the line was so clear that he could have been speaking to her from the next room.

'Where are you calling from?'

'I'm here at the hotel in New Ansbach,' he informed her, adding confusion to her concern. 'Do you think you could join me here for dinner this evening?'

'Yes, of course,' she agreed without hesitation, but her curiosity demanded to be satisfied. 'What are you doing here in New Ansbach?'

'I'll explain everything to you when I see you this evening,' he brusquely evaded her query. 'We could meet here in the hotel lounge at . . . shall we make it seven o'clock?'

'That would be perfect,' Maura agreed, mystified.

'I'll see you later then,' he ended the conversation abruptly, and Maura replaced the receiver with a bewildered expression on her face.

'You can stop worrying about leaving me alone at home this evening. My cousin is staying at the hotel in town, and he wants me to meet him there for dinner,' Maura explained when she strolled into the small kitchen where Joan was making a pot of tea. 'I wonder what's wrong.'

'Should there be something wrong?' Joan demanded gravely.

'Gavin and Clayton have never been the best of friends,' Maura answered her with a wry smile while she secured the towel around her head and seated herself at the table to add milk and sugar to the cup of tea which Joan had poured for her. 'They're complete opposites, except where their dedication to their work is concerned, and Gavin would never come to New Ansbach unless it's by invitation, so it has to be a matter of grave urgency.'

It was this knowledge that disturbed Maura most, and she was almost sick with concern that evening when she parked her Volkswagen at the entrance to the hotel.

'Maura!' Gavin smiled at her and rose from his chair close to the door when she entered the crowded hotel lounge. 'Thank you for coming,' he said, clasping both her hands in his and lowering his head to hers to kiss her proffered cheek.

'You have aroused my curiosity and my concern,' she told him when they were seated. 'It has to be something of grave importance to bring you here to New Ansbach.'

'Would you like something to drink before we go in to dinner?' he asked, heightening her anxiety by failing to comment on her remark.

'A sherry would be nice, thank you,' she agreed, clamping down on her impatience while he raised a hand to summon a hovering steward.

Gavin ordered a brandy for himself and a glass of sherry for Maura, and their conversation consisted of platitudes while they waited. She questioned him about his mother, and it was a relief to know that her aunt was in good health, but it merely intensified her curiosity as to the reason for her cousin's presence in New Ansbach.

'This isn't much of a hotel, is it,' Gavin remarked, casting a critical glance about the room, and not caring if the steward heard him when he approached them with their drinks and placed them on the low, circular table between their chairs.

'New Ansbach isn't on the tourist map, but this hotel has all the necessary amenities for travellers who need a place to stop over for the night,' Maura replied defensively when the steward had departed to serve someone else. 'If you wanted comfort you should have stayed the night at Hilltop House.'

'Heaven forbid!' Gavin pulled a face, and there was a hint of nervousness in the way he tried to pat his unruly fair hair into place. 'How is Angela?' he asked almost as an afterthought, gulping down a mouthful of brandy.

'She is well, thank you.' Maura took a sip of her sherry and observed her cousin closely. He was stalling instead of explaining the reason for this meeting, and she wondered at the reason for his odd behaviour.

'Clayton is still the same. I suppose.' Gavin's smile was mocking. 'Solid and dependable, and taking his responsibilities much too seriously for his own good.'

Maura did not reply to his remark. She disliked discussing Clayton with Gavin, most especially now, and she was becoming rather irritated by Gavin's evasive manner.

'Why have you come here to New Ansbach, Gavin?' she questioned him with a quiet determination to learn the truth, and she was surprised to glimpse a hint of anxiety in his blue eyes when she raised her glass to her lips and sipped at her sherry.

'I would like to suggest that we eat first and talk business later,' he answered her abruptly, and he drained his brandy glass with unnecessary haste.

'Business?' she echoed, her startled glance noticing for the first time the leather briefcase which stood on the floor beside his chair. 'If it's business you want to discuss, then shouldn't you be talking to Clayton?'

'My business is with you, Maura,' he assured her, rising to his feet. 'Shall we eat first?'

'Whatever you say,' she agreed, wondering if she looked as stunned as she was feeling at that moment when she rose to her feet and left the remainder of her sherry on the low table to accompany her cousin from the hotel lounge.

Gavin kept the conversation flowing in a casual direction while they dined in the spacious old dining-room with its high, pressed ceiling, pillared alcoves and glass doors set in Tudor arches which led out on to a wide *stoep* overlooking a well-kept garden which was floodlit at night. The hotel always served an excellent meal, and the dining-room was reasonably full that evening, but the diners were mostly local people whom Maura knew only by sight.

The waiter removed their empty dessert dishes while they finished off their meal with a cup of coffee, and Maura's patience had reached a point where it was about to disintegrate into anger.

'I hate to rush you, Gavin,' she brought the matter to a head when she pushed her empty cup aside, 'but I have a pile of work to get through this evening before I can go to bed, and it's getting late.'

'Would you like another cup of coffee?' he stalled again, but she shook her head firmly.

'No, thank you.'

The smile vanished from Gavin's ruggedly handsome face to leave it looking grim as they rose from the table and returned to the lounge where he ordered himself another brandy as if he needed a drink to boost his courage. This was not like Gavin at all, and her anxiety spiralled to an alarming peak.

'Maura, I can't tell you how much I hate having to do this, but there is no one else I can turn to for assistance,' he said at length, gulping down a mouthful of this drink and smiling twistedly. 'They say one should never do business with one's family, but then you know you can trust me. Don't you?'

'Yes, Gavin, I trust you,' she replied without hesitation. 'Tell me what's bothering you and how I may help.'

'It's this damned recession,' he explained at last, frowning down into the glass of amber liquid he held in his hand, and adding validity to the casual remark his mother had made on the telephone to Angela some weeks ago. 'The economic situation during the past couple of years has put my business under tremendous pressure, but it has survived, and the future is actually beginning to look a little rosier. What I need desperately at the moment is a financial boost to my liquid assets.'

Maura grasped the situation at once. 'You want me to lend you some money?'

'Yes,' Gavin nodded, looking embarrassed, 'but I would prefer you to consider it as an investment which will, after five years, be repaid—plus interest, of course.'

'How much?' she asked bluntly. 'How much do you need?'

'Two hundred thousand.'

Maura drew a careful breath and hid her surprise behind an outwardly calm expression. 'That's a lot of money.'

'I know,' he agreed grimly, draining his glass and opening his briefcase to produce a legal-looking document which he passed to her across the low table. 'If you need proof that this is legitimate, then I suggest you take a look at that. It's a certified copy of a document stating that my tender has been accepted for the erection of a large shopping-complex on the south coast, and they now require the usual ten per cent guarantee. I can't afford to let this contract slip through my fingers, but in recent years the economic recession caused an escalation in my general expenses, and I'm a bit short of liquid cash at the moment.' Maura looked up from her brief study of the document he had handed her, and she found him observing her with an urgent plea in his eyes. 'I can promise you that you won't lose on the deal, Maura.'

She knew enough about business to realise that he was speaking the truth, and she knew enough about her cousin's integrity to feel assured that he would never involve her in something from which she would not benefit.

'I'll help you, Gavin.' She wished that she could have left it at that, but she was incapable of ignoring the only obstacle in the path of her decision to give her cousin the financial help he required. 'You do understand, of course, that I shall have to mention this to Clayton before we can make any definite arrangements?'

'Yes, I understand, but——' There was a look of nervous anxiety on his face when he combed his fingers agitatedly through his fair hair. 'I think this is the part I dread most.'

'I know,' she murmured, her own anxiety escalating when she forced herself to face facts. 'Clayton has the power to nullify my agreement to help you.'

'How good are your powers of persuasion?'

'Pretty good in this instance, I think,' she smiled, her mind latching on to something which she hoped she could use as leverage. 'How soon do you need a definite answer?'

'I must have an answer within forty-eight hours,' he said, 'and you can keep that copy of the document stating that my tender has been accepted if you think it will help at all to convince Clayton that this is legit.'

'Where shall I contact you?' she asked when Gavin accompanied her out to where she had parked her car at the well lit entrance to the hotel.

'I'm leaving here before breakfast tomorrow morning, so it will have to be at my office, or at home.'

'You'll hear from me,' she promised, reaching up to

kiss him on the cheek before she unlocked the door of
her Volkswagen and slipped in behind the wheel.
'Thanks for the dinner, Gavin, and give my love to
Aunt Fiona,' she said, closing the door and winding
down the window.

'Maura . . .' He had to stoop to bring his face on a
level with hers when she turned the key in the ignition to
start the car, and his expression was sombre when he
took her hand off the steering-wheel and held it in his
own. 'Regardless of what happens . . . thank you.'

Maura squeezed his fingers affectionately before he
released her hand and stepped away from her car, and
her mind was churning madly when she drove through
the quiet streets towards the cottage on the northern
outskirts of the town.

She could imagine Clayton's reaction when she told
him about Gavin's request, but she could not risk
predicting the possibility of her victory. It would depend
on the strength of her 'powers of persuasion', and she
had very little time in which to prepare herself for yet
another clash of wills.

'No! It's absolutely out of the question!' Clayton's
explosive reaction was exactly as Maura had imagined it
would be when she confronted him, by appointment this
time, in his office at Fieldco the following afternoon.
'Under no circumstances will I allow you to lend Gavin
Porter a sum of money like that!'

'The money is there, Clayton,' Maura argued hotly as
they stood glaring at each other with the width of his
mahogany desk between them. 'It's available at a
moment's notice, and it is mine to do with as I please.'

'Only if you have my approval,' he stripped her
argument down to the bone, 'and in this instance you do
not!'

'I'm not asking the impossible, and I have enough business sense to know that I'm not throwing good money away on a floundering cause,' she persisted. 'Why don't you trust my judgement just this once?'

Clayton gestured disparagingly and lit a cigarette. 'Your judgement is based on the fact that Gavin Porter is your cousin,' he said scathingly, 'and you are such a trusting little idiot that it wouldn't surprise me to learn that you never thought to ask for the necessary proof to corroborate his story.'

He was not only insulting her, he was casting doubt on her integrity and intelligence, and her resentment flared sharply.

'Proof? You want proof?' Her grey eyes sparked with fury when she found the document she was looking for in her briefcase, and slammed it down on the desk in front of Clayton. 'Here is proof! Go on, *read* it!'

The atmosphere was very tense, and Clayton's dark, angry gaze held hers for an electrifying second before he picked up the document and glanced through it.

'This is merely an acceptance of Gavin's tender, and it's insufficient as a guarantee that he will be in a financial position to pay back the loan in five years' time.'

This was true, Maura could not deny it, but she was not going to admit defeat without putting up a reasonable argument.

'I know you're not too crazy about Gavin as a person, but you have to admit that he's an astute businessman, and that he wouldn't be foolish enough to do anything which might jeopardise the company which he had to build up from scratch after his father's death. Oh, come on, Clayton!' she laughed derisively, pitting her determination and her wit against his when she glimpsed a slight softening in the stubborn, unrelenting set of his jaw. 'If you were prepared to spend two hundred thousand on a car which I didn't want, and never asked for, then you have no cause to deny me the right to help my cousin financially.'

'That's moral blackmail,' he laughed unexpectedly, and she was suddenly stripped of the shield of her anger to find herself exposed to the awe-inspiring magnetism of this man who held her heart in the palm of his hand.

'It's the truth,' she insisted as she watched him put out his cigarette and walk round the desk to stand less than a pace away from her.

He had not come this close to her since that night when he had joined her on the window-seat in her room to listen to the nightjar, and she could not control her pulse when they responded to his nearness with a wild leap.

'You've lost weight,' he said with brotherly concern, his dark glance sliding over her critically and lingering on the ultra-slender curves of her body in the crisp white blouse and grey and blue striped skirt.

'I've been rather busy lately.' She brushed aside his remark, her breathing suddenly restricted as she turned away from him and busied herself with snapping shut the locks on her briefcase.

'You need a break,' he announced in a voice which she imagined was similar to that of a doctor prescribing treatment to a patient. 'I have to go down to Durban for a couple of days in July. The trip coincides with the school holidays, and it might be a good idea if you accompanied me. A few relaxing days on the beach might bring the colour back into your cheeks and put a little more flesh on your body.'

'That . . . would be . . . nice,' she agreed haltingly, tempted by the enticing thought of lazy days on the sun-baked sands, and sultry nights . . .! No! She dared not let her mind wander into forbidden territory. 'About the loan.' She hastily steered the conversation on to safer ground, and Clayton's sensuous mouth tightened with a hint of displeasure.

'I shall have to take time to consider it.'

Time! Her stomach twisted itself into a knot of anxiety. Time was running out on Gavin, and he could not afford the delay which she was beginning to envisage.

'I need your answer not later than this evening.'

Clayton frowned down at her angrily. 'Don't put pressure on me, Maura.'

'I don't mean to pressurise you, but it is rather an urgent matter,' she persisted, adopting a cautious and congenial manner for Gavin's sake more than her own. 'And you *will* give me an answer this evening, won't you?' she added, holding her breath mentally.

Clayton observed her with a frowning intensity for several frightening seconds before he moved his wide shoulders in a gesture of irritation beneath the confining cotton of his shirt. 'I'll call you,' he said abruptly, stepping round his desk to resume his seat.

Maura sighed inwardly with relief, but she knew that she still had a few anxious hours ahead of her. She thanked him and left, afraid that, if she lingered, she might say something to make him reject her request without consideration, and she did not want that to happen.

She could not settle down to anything during the remainder of that afternoon, and she jumped at every sound, her nervous agitation almost causing her to ruin their dinner. What had Clayton decided? Why didn't he call? Did he have to make her wait until her nerves had been stretched to breaking point?

'What's the matter with you?' Joan demanded

humorously that evening when Maura paced the kitchen floor restlessly after they had washed and packed away their dinner dishes. 'You're as fidgety as a kitten, and you've done almost everything except bite your nails.'

'I'm sorry, Joan.' Maura pulled out a chair and sat down heavily, her frowning glance resting on the pile of books in front of her which still had to be marked that evening. 'I'm expecting a call from Clayton about that loan Gavin wants, and I'm hoping that he'll agree with what I want to do, but the waiting is killing me.'

Joan smiled sympathetically. 'You can't blame Clayton if he's taking time to investigate the matter before giving you an answer.'

'But it doesn't *need* to be investigated, and I don't see why he can't——'

The shrill ring of the telephone cut across Maura's angry protestation, and she hesitated only a fraction of a second before she leapt to her feet and stormed out of the kitchen to answer it.

'Maura, it's Clayton,' that familiar gravelly voice seemed to growl into her ear, and her anxiety escalated sharply.

'Yes?' she answered him abruptly, incapable in that instance of raising her own voice above a whisper while she waited for him to reveal his direction.

'You can go ahead,' he said, giving her the answer she had prayed for all afternoon and evening.

She could, however, scarcely believe her victory and, almost faint with relief, she closed her eyes and slumped weakly into the armchair beside the telephone table.

'Thank you, Clayton,' she croaked in gratitude. 'Thank you very much.'

'Don't thank me,' he warned darkly. 'I'm trusting your judgement in this matter, so I sugget you pray that this venture works out for you.'

Their conversation ended on that warning note, but Maura had no doubts about her decision to help Gavin. It was an investment from which she would finally reap a reward.

She was on the telephone for the next fifteen minutes, talking to a very relieved Gavin, and discussing the arrangements which would have to be made for the transfer of the money.

'I can't thank you enough, Maura, and you won't regret it,' Gavin said before he rang off, and Maura sat there in the lounge for some time afterwards, hugging her excitement to herself.

She had not felt quite so alive in weeks. It had surprised her to learn that Clayton had sanctioned the loan on the basis of *her* judgement, and, in the process, he had succeeded in making her feel as if she had, at last, achieved something. Dear, wonderful, cautious Clayton. How very difficult it must have been for him to relinquish his powers in this instance and, oh, how she loved him for it.

Joan looked up when Maura walked into the kitchen, and she pushed her work aside with an amused twinkle in her eyes. 'From the look on your face I gather your decision has been okayed.'

'Yes, Clayton has agreed to the loan,' Maura smiled, seating herself at the table, and her grey eyes were sparkling with delight when her glance met Joan's.

'Well, good for Clayton!' Joan smiled wryly. 'In agreeing to your decision he has notched up yet another victory.'

Maura laughed humorously. 'I thought *I* was the one who had scored a victory.'

'I'm referring to his victory in gaining a stronger hold on your heart,' Joan explained, her expression suddenly grave. 'When are you going to do something about it,

Maura?'

The smile faded from Maura's face and she lowered her pain-filled eyes. 'In my clumsy way I did try to do something about it when I was home for the holidays,' she confided in Joan for the first time.

'And?' Joan prompted.

'I was told in no uncertain manner to behave myself,' Maura laughed shortly, biting down hard on her quivering lip, and blinking back the tears. 'Clayton loves me, but not—not in the way I want him to love me.'

'Rubbish!' Joan exclaimed sharply, brushing aside Maura's statement with an angry wave of her hand. 'I spoke out of turn once before, but this time I don't think you'll find it so upsetting to hear what I have to say. I saw the way Clayton looked at you that night when he came here to get your signature on those papers, and what I saw had nothing to do with brotherly love . . . *believe me!*'

Maura wanted desperately to believe Joan. It would be so very easy to believe her, but she could not bear the thought of being disillusioned again. 'You must have been mistaken,' she said dully.

'Oh, no, I was not!' Joan insisted adamantly. 'I've seen that look in a man's eyes before, and I'm telling you that Clayton loves you.'

'*Don't,* Joan,' she pleaded, her misery deepening. '*Please* don't make me hope again for something which I know I can never have.'

'I'm going to give you some advice, and it's up to you whether you take it or not'. Joan got up and switched on the electric kettle to make a pot of tea and, when she turned, she pinned Maura to her chair with a steady, challenging glance. 'Find out why Clayton is denying his feelings for you and, when you know the reason, you'll also know how to deal with the barriers he has erected.'

Maura did not answer her. The barriers which Clayton had erected were impregnable, and she was not going to humiliate herself again by attempting to bring them down. If Clayton loved her, as Joan insisted he did, then it was up to him to make the next move.

CHAPTER SEVEN

MAURA smiled inwardly when she stood and watched the children file out of the classroom on the last day of that second term. They were having difficulty in suppressing their excitement at the thought of the three-week holiday which lay ahead of them, and Maura's smile deepened when she recalled her own childhood elation at the end of each term. Oh, if only she could feel that way again.

'Have a nice holiday, Miss Fielding,' one of the children said to her in passing.

Have a nice holiday? Maura groaned inwardly. She was not looking forward to these three weeks at home and, most of all, she dreaded the few days she would have to spend in Durban with Clayton. She had not wanted to go, but the expansions to the mill necessitated the purchase of extra machinery and equipment, and Clayton had insisted that her presence, as major shareholder in Fieldco, would be preferable to her signature at the bottom of a letter of agreement.

Maura emerged from her disturbing thoughts to find herself alone in the classroom, and she sighed heavily as she picked up her briefcase and walked the length of the corridor to the staff-room to collect the jacket she had left there earlier that morning.

The staff-room was empty except for the Principal, who turned from the noticeboard to glance at Maura over the dark-rimmed reading-glasses perched on the tip of his beak-like nose, and his thin mouth curved in a smile. 'I want you to know that I'm very happy with your work, Miss Fielding.'

Maura fumbled in surprise when she lifted her jacket off the stand. Praise from this dear but crusty old man was something rare, and it had come at a time when she desperately needed something to lift her out of her depressed mood.

'Why, thank you, Mr Seymour,' she smiled back at him and, for want of anything better to say, she echoed the words which had been spoken to her minutes earlier. 'Have a nice holiday,' she said, walking out of the staff-room with a lightness in her step which had not been there before.

Maura was humming to herself when she arrived at the cottage. She said goodbye to Joan and Will when they left for Pietermaritzburg to spend the holiday with Joan's parents and, when they drove away, she loaded her suitcases into her Volkswagen and locked up the cottage. Maura was still humming to herself when she drove out to Fieldco, but she sobered when she glanced in the rear-view mirror to see Clayton's white Jaguar coming up behind her as she sped up the long driveway towards the pillared entrance to Hilltop House.

Her heart was thudding heavily against her ribs when she got out of her car, and she had to quell the ridiculous desire to turn and run when she saw him walk towards her. His dark grey suit was impeccably tailored, as always, to accentuate his wide-shouldered, long-limbed frame, and she could not prevent her senses from responding to that aura of maleness which surrounded him. She swallowed nervously and concentrated on his striped tie in an attempt to control the wild leaping of her pulses.

'Welcome home.' He kissed the top of her corn-gold head and, placing a casual arm about her waist, he accompanied her inside while one of the servants scurried out of the house to take care of her suitcases.

Maura glanced up at him curiously, her eyes narrowed against the glare of the sun. 'You don't usually arrive home at this time of the day.'

'Mother has been called out this afternoon to an emergency meeting of one of her charities, and we couldn't have you coming home to an empty house. Now could we?'

His smile was teasing, reminding her of the days when there had been no tension between them, and her mouth curved in an answering smile. 'I don't think it would have killed me to spend a few hours alone at home.'

'I thought I'd take the afternoon off, but if you'd prefer me to return to the office, then you only have to say so.'

'Oh, don't be silly!' she laughed as they paused in the hall, and she aimed a playful punch at his jaw, but his arm tensed about her waist when her knuckles brushed against his chin. Her expression sobered as she tilted her head back to encounter the dark, probing intensity of his eyes. The powerful tug of his magnetism quickened her pulse and, knowing that she did not have the strength to cope with the situation, she eased herself out of the circle of his arm. 'I could do with a long, cool drink,' she said, her voice deceptively light and casual as she preceded him into the living-room.

'So could I,' he agreed, walking towards the drinks cabinet. 'What will you have?'

'Soda with a dash of lime, thanks.'

Maura needed time to control the tremors inside her, and she walked across the room to stand in front of the window while Clayton poured their drinks. She stared out across the sunlit garden which had sadly not been left untouched by the coldness of the winter nights. All except the evergreen trees had shed their leaves, and an early frost had long since robbed the beautiful lawn of its greenness.

She pushed her hands into her wide skirt pockets, and her fingers encountered the letter from Will Baker which had been delivered to her classroom during the course of the morning. She had slipped it into her pocket, intending to read it later, and somehow she had not given it another thought. She opened the letter now and read it quickly.

'Maura, dear lady,' Will had written in typical theatrical style. 'This is going to be a holiday to remember. Patience is a commodity I no longer possess, and I want you to know that I am going to risk all on the altar by asking Joan to marry me. If the answer is "yes", I shall send you the biggest bunch of flowers I can lay my hands on. Love, Will.'

She turned at the sound of a step behind her, and she was convinced that she was smiling inanely when she met Clayton's mocking glance. 'Is that a letter from an admirer?' he asked, placing a tall glass of soda and lime in her hand, and she took a refreshing sip before she explained.

'It's a letter from Will Baker.'

Clayton's eyebrows rose in surprise, and a disapproving look flashed across his lean face. 'I thought he was courting Joan.'

'Oh, but he *is!* Here,' she smiled, holding out the letter for his inspection, 'read it.'

Clayton was oddly hesitant when he took the letter from her to read it, and his glance was curious when he handed it back to her. 'Why should he want to send you flowers?'

'I suppose it's because I . . . well, I paved the way for him a little with Joan.' Maura's smile deepened at the memory. 'Joan had quite a few preconceived notions about Will, and she had erected such a vicious barrier that the poor man couldn't get anywhere near her.'

Clayton's expression cleared. 'So you played Cupid?'

'Not exactly,' she laughed, slipping Will's letter into her pocket and walking away from Clayton's disturbing nearness to lower herself into a comfortably padded armchair. 'When do we leave for Durban?' She changed the subject hastily when Clayton seated himself in a chair close to her own.

'Today in two weeks' time,' he said, loosening his tie and swallowing down a mouthful of Coke.

'That's on a Friday,' Maura commented in surprise. 'You can't possibly get everything done in one day, and no one will open up shop over a weekend.'

'I wasn't planning on us doing anything in particular until the Monday.' His sensuous mouth curved in a faintly mocking smile. 'I did promise you a couple of lazy days on the beach, didn't I?'

'Yes, you did,' she murmured, recalling his promise with great clarity and not quite sure whether she liked the idea of an idle weekend in Durban with Clayton for company.

'Are you looking forward to it?'

'Yes . . . and, no,' she answered him truthfully, trailing her finger absently along the rim of her glass.

'What's that supposed to mean?'

'*Yes,* I'm looking forward to lazing on the beach and, *no,* I'm not looking forward to the business side of the trip.'

'That's something you'll have to get used to, since I intend you to become a great deal more involved in the business side of Fieldco,' he informed her in a clipped voice, and she glanced up at him sharply.

'I'm a teacher, Clayton,' she reminded him coldly. 'I

don't have a degree in business economics, and the little I know about lumber isn't worth mentioning.'

'You could learn if you put your mind to it.'

'No.' She shook her head adamantly and drank thirstily from her glass.

'Maura, I'm not asking you to resign your job as a teacher to sit behind a desk at Fieldco,' he explained tolerantly, 'but I would appreciate it if you could show a little more interest in the business side of a company which is as much yours as it is Mother's and mine.'

The clock on the mantelshelf chimed three, and it jarred her nerves while she sipped thoughtfully at her soda and lime drink. Clayton was making her feel guilty, and she resented it.

'In what way would you want me to show an interest?'

'You could sit in on some of our meetings, and you could read the monthly reports I send to you instead of throwing them away unopened,' he suggested, his accuracy startling her and intensifying her feeling of guilt.

'What makes you think that I throw them away unopened?' she questioned him cautiously, wondering how he had discovered the truth.

'I enclosed a message with last month's report, and you never responded to it,' he explained accusingly.

'Oh!' Maura's cheeks flamed with embarrassment, but she made no attempt to deny the truth. 'What was the message?' she asked curiously.

There was a gleam of derisive mockery in the eyes that met hers over the rim of his glass. 'I had to meet someone in town on business, and I invited you to join me for dinner afterwards, if you were free.'

Maura's initial surprise ended in a stab of regret. 'Oh, Clayton, I'm sorry.'

'And so you should be!' he admonished her with a twisted smile. 'How about a game of tennis to make up for it,' he suggested, draining his glass of Coke.

'That's a great idea,' she agreed hastily, finishing the remainder of her drink and rising hastily to her feet. 'Let's go up and change.'

They arranged to meet at the tennis court, and Maura hurried to her room to haul her tennis gear out of her wardrobe. She dressed quickly, exchanging her skirt and blouse for shorts and a T-shirt, and her sandals for tennis shoes. She tied back her hair with a blue scarf to keep it out of her face, and if she had paused long enough in front of the mirror she might have noticed that her features had come alive for the first time in weeks.

Her heart was racing for some obscure reason when she arrived at the tennis court to find Clayton putting up the net. He looked magnificent in white tennis shorts and open-necked shirt, and she stood for a moment admiring the play of muscles in his sun-browned arms and legs. It was only when he looked up and saw her that she went down the steps on to the tennis court to help him, but she found that she was so intensely aware of his maleness that she was almost clumsy in her efforts to assist him.

Damn him for having this effect on her! She cursed him in silence when they left the court to collect their rackets and tennis balls.

Maura was a strong player, but she was no match for Clayton. He beat her six games to two, and they were both perspiring freely when they finally walked off the court.

'Your game has improved,' Clayton announced, dropping his racket on to the grass, and wiping his face and hands on a small towel while he seated himself on the corner of the wooden table beneath the shady oak tree.

'I'll take that as a compliment considering that I haven't played much tennis since I left college,' she laughed breathlessly, placing her racket on the table and sitting down heavily on the wooden bench which circled the tree. She was dabbing at her own face and neck with her towel when their glances met unexpectedly, and she saw something in his eyes that made her discard her towel and lean back against the gnarled stem of the tree. 'What's on your mind, Clayton?' she asked quietly, and his mouth twitched with a suggestion of a smile.

'We're at a disadvantage, you and I. We know each other too well for one to hoodwink the other.'

Maura felt a nervous tug at her insides. 'I agree that we have a reasonable surface knowledge of each other.'

'I know you better that that, Maura.' He laughed shortly, his glance lingering on the rapid rise and fall of her small breasts and dropping lower to her tanned, shapely legs stretched out in front of her.

'How can you?' she protested warily, aware of an extra warmth surging into her cheeks which had nothing to do with physical exertion. 'I don't share all my thoughts and feelings with you.'

'You don't have to. You have very expressive eyes, and at this very moment you're afraid, but the question is . . . are you afraid of me, or are you afraid of yourself, Kitten?'

He startled her with the use of that half-forgotten pet name, and his probing glance held hers with an intensity that made her feel as if he was attempting to strip her down to her soul.

It was true . . . she *was* afraid! She was afraid of those feelings he could arouse simply by being in the same room with her, and she was afraid of what he might discover if he should probe too deeply. She was also angry. How could he remain so detached while every nerve in her body was aroused to a tingling alertness whenever he came near her!

'I think you wanted to discuss something with me,' She steered the conversation back in the direction she had initially intended it to go, and Clayton nodded amiably.

'It's about Gavin,' he began, and Maura was instantly on the defensive.

'Look, I know you don't like him very much, but——'

'Let me finish!' Clayton interrupted her sharply, and Maura lapsed into silence to allow him to continue. 'I know you're not going to like this, but I had your cousin investigated purely as a formality, and I've received some disturbing news which I feel you ought to know about. Gavin has landed himself a multi-million-rand contract, and to do this he has indebted himself not only to you, but also to his bank. Porter & Son is a small company, and some might say it is ill-equipped to cope with such a vast undertaking. If he crashes on this deal it could wipe him out.'

'I was aware of the risk involved when I agreed to help Gavin financially. Oh, don't look so disapproving, Clayton!' she rebuked him sharply. 'I may not know much about business, but I do know that success isn't something which can be achieved without risk. Didn't my father and yours risk *everything* they possessed to make a success of Fieldco?'

'That was thirty years ago, Maura.'

'A risk is still a risk,' she insisted. 'I believe Gavin is very much aware of what he might lose if he fails in this venture, but he also knows what he will gain if he succeeds, and that is what he is aiming at.'

Clayton's expression became inscrutable, and he observed her in silence for several interminable seconds before he said, 'You obviously have great faith in Gavin's ability to succeed.'

'I have faith in the people I love and trust because I know they will never let me down if they can help it.' She stared down at the yellowed oak-tree leaf which had fluttered down on to the bench beside her, and she picked it up to run it absently through her fingers. 'I feel the same way about you.'

Maura held her breath mentally, afraid suddenly that she might have said too much, but Clayton did not comment on her remark, and her taut body began to relax.

'You make life seem so simple,' he laughed cynically.

'Life *is* simple.' Her grey glance was unwavering when it met his. 'We are basically the creators of our own problems, and then we don't always know how to solve them.'

'Have you created a problem for yourself recently which you don't know how to solve?' he asked her, driving her into a mental corner with the familiar gleam of mockery in his eyes.

'Yes, I have,' she admitted cautiously, her mind latching on to the painful problem she had created for herself by falling in love with this man who preferred to continue thinking of her as his sister. 'What about you?'

'I can't deny that I have created a problem for myself.' Clayton's compelling glance captured hers and held it. 'What have you done about yours?'

'I've put mine on ice in the hope that I might find an answer some time in the near future,' she confessed with a growing sense of alarm at the feeling that their discussion was no longer objective. 'And you?' she could not help asking.

'I've done the same.'

'You surprise me, Clayton,' she laughed, attempting

to ease that sudden and inexplicable tension between them. 'I have always thought of you as someone who knew all the answers.'

'Disappointed?' he mocked her.

'No.' She shook her head, her expression sobering. 'It makes you human.'

One heavy eyebrow was arched in sardonic amusement. 'Have I appeared inhuman to you, Kitten?'

There it was again. *Kitten.* Why, after all these years, was he calling her by that name again?

'I've never thought of you as inhuman,' she corrected him hastily when she had gathered her scattered wits about her. 'But I have thought of you as infallible.'

His sensuous mouth curved in a bone-melting smile as he leaned towards her to trail a lazy finger along the curve of her hot cheek. 'I have been known to make mistakes, you know.'

Clayton's eyes mocked her one instant, and the next they appeared to be demanding something of her which she dared not give. What did he think he was doing? He was the one who had drawn the dividing line between them with the stern instruction that she must never attempt to cross it, and now he was tempting her to do exactly what he had warned her against. His fingers were trailing a sensually destructive path down to the hollow of her throat where her pulse was beating erratically, and she was besieged with the mad desire to take his hand and guide it down to her breast where her nipples had hardened in anticipation. Oh, God, why was he tormenting her like this?

'I'm going to take a shower before Mother returns home.' She got up jerkily to escape his touch, and his mouth tightened as if in anger.

'Good idea,' he said abruptly.

They collected their things and walked in silence,

taking the path which led up to the house through the surrounding trees, and Maura cast a quick, nervous glance at Clayton's rigid profile. What had she done to annoy him? Or was it possible that he could be annoyed with himself? Maura sighed inwardly. If this was an indication of what she could expect from Clayton, then she was dreading those few days alone with him in Durban.

Maura drew the curtains aside at the window of her suite in a beach-front hotel and stared out across the restless Indian ocean. They had motored down to Durban that afternoon in Clayton's Jaguar, and within a few minutes she would be meeting him in the hotel lounge for a drink before dinner.

The moon was rising higher in the dark, velvety sky, and coloured lights flickered brightly in the amusement arcade across the street. There were people wherever she looked. They were revelling in Durban's warm, humid climate and the near-festive atmosphere which prevailed at the coast at that time of the year, but Maura felt oddly distanced from their gaiety, and her thoughts drifted elsewhere.

A large bouquet of yellow chrysanthemums had been delivered to Maura at Hilltop House during the second week of the July holiday, and the accompanying note had read: 'We're going to be married. I would have preferred a quiet, immediate ceremony, but, alas, it's going to be a December wedding. Love, Will.'

The telephone had almost vibrated with Joan's happiness and excitement when Maura had called to congratulate them, and the memory of that conversation made the corners of Maura's generous mouth quiver into a faintly melancholy smile. She was very happy for them, but there was no sense in denying that her happiness for Joan was also accompanied by an undeniable twinge of envy. Joan had finally made a bid for the man she wanted, and she had got him. Maura wished that she could do the same with Clayton, but her first tentative bid had been so fiercely rejected that she did not dare risk it again.

She sighed heavily as she glanced at her wrist watch, and the silky folds of her cool blue dress swayed gently about her legs when she turned from the window with a jerky movement to collect her evening purse in the bedroom. She wished that she could have lingered a moment longer, but it was time to go downstairs, and she knew from experience that Clayton disliked to be kept waiting.

He rose from his chair when she entered the magnificent lounge with its mirrored walls reflecting the potted palms and leafy ferns, and he looked tall and impressive in is dark evening suit. Maura's pulse-rate quickened, but her heartbeats subsided with a dull ache when she glimpsed a look of envy in the eyes of an attractive redhead seated nearby. 'Oh, you have no cause to envy me,' Maura could have told her. 'Clayton is free, and there is no possibility that he will ever belong to me.' This had leapt into Maura's mind as an added warning, and her heart felt like lead in her breast. The burden of her hopeless yearning was fast becoming too much for her to bear.

'You look enchanting, Maura.' Clayton smiled at her with an unexpected warmth in his eyes, and her breath caught in her throat when his glance shifted slowly down her slender body and up again to linger on the diamond pendant which sparkled against her creamy skin. 'I have taken the liberty of ordering a sherry for you,' he said when they were seated.

'Thank you,' she murmured her approval, an embarrassing warmth invading her cheeks when she saw his glance shift to where the low neckline of her dress exposed the shadowy cleft between her breasts, and her heart was suddenly beating so fast that she was finding it difficult to breathe normally.

Clayton continued to look at her with that strange warmth in his dark eyes. It was confusing and disconcerting, and she was clinging tightly to her evening purse to still the tremor in her hands when the bar steward created a timely diversion by arriving with their drinks.

Maura took a sip of sherry to steady those quivering nerves at the pit of her stomach, but it did nothing to lessen her awareness of those eyes which were observing every movement she made.

'Was there anything in particular you wanted to do after dinner this evening?' Clayton asked, the tinkling of the ice in his whisky glass jarring her sensitive nerves when he raised his glass to his lips.

'I haven't planned anything, but it's obvious that you have something in mind,' she replied, taking a second sip of sherry and succeeding somehow in regaining a fraction of her composure.

'I do have something in mind, but it's nothing strenuous,' he confessed. 'I was thinking of a short stroll along the promenade before we retired for the night, and I'm hoping that the sea air might blow away some of the cobwebs.'

'Cobwebs?' she echoed curiously.

'The past two weeks at the mill have been strenuous, and my head feels as if it has become clogged with sawdust.' He smiled faintly and lowered his gaze to the glass she was clutching so tightly in her hand. 'Perhaps you need to relax as well.'

'I *am* relaxed.'

'No, you're not, Maura,' he contradicted her mockingly, his eyes still on the glass which had jolted visibly in her hand at the accuracy with which he had diagnosed her present state of mind and body. 'You're so tense that you're liable to crack if someone were to come up behind you and say *boo*.'

Her cheeks flamed and, disconcerted by his remark, she drank her sherry much too fast. It hit her empty stomach like a ball of fire, but the shock of it seemed to have the desired effect on her nerves.

'I wis you could be a little less observant.'

'I shall wear blinkers in future,' he promised with a mock gravity which made the corners of her soft mouth lift in amusement. 'Ah, at last! You're smiling, and when you smile your eyes light up and sparkle like jewels.'

Her smile faded when his compelling glance captured hers once again, and her pulses throbbed with a pagan rhythm when she found herself trapped in the smouldering darkness of his eyes. Everything else in the hotel lounge seemed to fade into the shadows . . . leaving only Clayton and herself, and that curious sensation that they had become linked by a cable of communication which required no words.

There was an element of danger in this uncanny situation which had developed between them. Maura was alerted to something in him which contradicted his statement of a few months ago that he had no intention of deviating from their brother/sister relationship. He had kissed her that night in his study, and she knew that he had enjoyed it, but he had rejected her afterwards with a savagery which she would never forget. She had walked into a trap of her own making that night, but she was not going to do it again. It had hurt too much, and it would hurt a great deal more now.

It was the memory of that painful experience that helped her to sever this odd link between them. 'If you weren't my brother I'd think you were flirting with me,' she said, injecting a note of mockery into her voice.

'If you weren't my sister, then I might have said you're correct in your assumption,' he countered with an equal dose of mockery, his glance holding hers relentlessly until he lowered his gaze to her soft, pink mouth, and Maura's lips tingled as if she had actually been kissed.

'This sherry has gone to my head.' She laughed away the crazy sensations spiralling through her. 'When do we eat?'

'Right now, if you like,' he replied, smiling at her in a way which aroused a suffocating suspicion that he knew exactly what she was thinking and feeling, and her heart raced madly in her breast while he put out his cigarette and finished his drink.

The hotel's *à la carte* restaurant catered to every desire of every individual diner. The menu contained a mouth-watering variety of dishes from which to choose, but Maura was too tense and nervous to order a heavy meal, and she settled for a grilled sole and salads while Clayton ordered club rump for himself.

A bottle of wine was brought to their table while they waited. Their glasses were filled, but Maura took no more than one sip. Her head was still spinning with those intoxicating flights of fancy aroused by the sherry she had swallowed down in such haste, and she knew that it would be dangerous for her to drink another drop of alcohol before she had eaten something.

She had become incredibly nervous and tense, and she searched frantically for something to say during the ensuing silence. There was so much she *could* have said to him, but her mind was a jumble of thoughts and feelings which dared not be voiced. She was relieved when their meal was served, and it was Clayton who eased the tension between them by discussing with her the business side of their visit to Durban.

Maura forced herself to concentrate on what he was saying, and she somehow succeeded in divesting her mind of everything else. They talked at length while they ate, discussing the expansions to the mill and the new machinery and equipment which had to be bought, and Maura gradually began to relax in his company.

It was ridiculous to think that she could allow herself to become so tense in the presence of someone whom she had known all her life. Her adoration as a child had not hampered their relationship, but her love for him as a woman had created an awkward barrier between them which was emotionally as uncomfortable as the braces she had worn as a child to straighten her teeth.

Dammit! Why had life become so complicated for her? Why could everything not have remained the same as it used to be in the past?

'Do you dance, Maura?' Clayton asked unexpectedly when they were finishing off their meal with a cup of coffee, and her startled glance met his across the candle-lit table.

'You know I do.'

'I know you move very nicely to the wild, modern music they play these days,' he smiled at her, the flickering flame of the candle adding a touch of devilment to his appearance. 'What about an old-fashioned two-step.'

Amusement lurked in her eyes, and she tilted her head in an unconsciously coquettish manner. 'Are you asking me to dance with you, Clayton?'

'I am,' he said, reaching for her hand across the table and drawing her to her feet before she could refuse.

'I'm not very good at this,' she warned him nervously when they reached that small section of the floor which had been cleared for dancing, and which was rapidly becoming crowded with dancing couples.

'There's nothing to it.' Clayton smiled as he slid his hand about her waist until it rested in the small of her rigid back. 'All you have to do is relax.'

'I *am* relaxed,' she argued untruthfully when he guided her across the floor in time to the slow beat of the dreamy tune the band was playing.

'No, you're not!'

'Let's not start that again.' She laughed off the tension which seemed to be gripping every muscle in her body.

'You don't have to be nervous with me, Kitten,' he mocked her. 'You're quite safe.'

Safe? The word echoed derisively through her mind. Oh, yes, she was *safe* with Clayton, but it was herself she was concerned about. How safe was she when he could arouse such tempestuous feelings inside her, and how good was she at disguising them?

Her hand tightened defensively on Clayton's shoulder when he drew her closer unexpectedly to avoid a collision with another couple on the floor. He murmured an apology, his warm breath fanning her temple, but his arm did not slacken about her waist, and neither did she protest when he continued to hold her so that their bodies touched and swayed together as one on the floor.

Maura's heart was thudding in her breast, and her emotions were running riot. To be this close to Clayton was more potent than the glass of wine she had had with her dinner. It dulled her mind, and gave her body the freedom to enjoy the sensual delight of this physical contact for as long as it might last. His steps were easy to follow, and she relaxed at last to surrender herself to the magic of this moment.

She wished that this dance would never end and, as if to fulfil her silent wish, the band played on, their music flowing from one song into another, but logic began to intrude on her state of euphoria. From the hidden depths of her subconscious came the warning that she was allowing herself to drift into a situation which she might not be able to control, and it left her considerably sobered when the dance finally ended.

'Do you realise that this is the first time we've danced together?' she asked with a defensive flippancy she had dragged up from somewhere when Clayton escorted her back to their table.

'The opportunity has never been there before.' There was a strange look in his eyes which she could not interpret, and there was an even stranger tension in him which seemed to flow through her like a current of electricity from the hand that cupped her elbow. 'Shall we go for that walk?'

Maura nodded in agreement when an extraordinary tightness gripped her throat and prevented her from speaking, and they left the hotel restaurant in silence.

CHAPTER EIGHT

THE sun was blazing down on to the crowded beach from a near cloudless sky on the Saturday morning, and Maura closed her eyes against its blinding brilliance as she lay back on the towel she had spread out on the sand. She was aware of Clayton's tanned, muscular frame stretched out on a towel beside her, but she felt comfortably relaxed. She had had a restful night, the first in weeks, and she was not sure who to credit for that luxury.

Her thoughts wandered back to the events of the previous evening, and she could almost laugh at herself when she remembered how wary she had been of Clayton at the start of that leisurely walk along the promenade, but the feeling had passed swiftly. He had taken her hand when they had crossed the busy, well lit street, and her hand had somehow remained in his while they had strolled in companionable silence among the many holidaymakers who had shared their desire for a walk along the promenade before retiring for the night. Later, when an unexpected nip in the air had made her shiver, Clayton had draped his jacket about her shoulders. She had hugged it about her, loving the feel of the warmth of his body which had still clung to it, and she had returned it to him somewhat reluctantly when they had arrived back at the hotel.

Maura had felt pleasantly tired when Clayton had unlocked the door to her suite, and she had most certainly not expected his goodnight kiss. She had looked up,

131

intending to thank him for the enjoyable evening, but he had lowered his head at that precise moment, and his kiss, intended for her cheek, had landed on her soft lips. They had both been startled, and then amused by the incident, but his second kiss had been aimed deliberately at her lips before he had walked away from her to enter the adjoining suite.

'Why are you smiling?'

Clayton's gravelly voice startled her back to the present to make her aware of the fact that he had been observing her, and she did not risk looking at him while she fought desperately to control the rapid beat of her heart.

'I'm not smiling at anything in particular,' she replied evasively.

It was the clanging of the ice-cream vendor's bell which finally made her open her eyes to discover that Clayton lay facing her, and he lifted himself up on one elbow when their glances met.

'Would you like an ice-cream?' he asked, smiling down into her eyes which were narrowed against the glare of the sun, and she shook her head.

'Ice-cream is fattening.'

'You could do with a bit more flesh on your body.' His dark, disturbing glance trailed over her bikini-clad body and lingered for an unnecessary length of time on the gentle, alluring curve of her breasts and hips. 'You are much too thin, Kitten.'

'Don't call me *Kitten!*' Maura protested, turning over on to her stomach to bury her hot face in her arms.

'Why not?'

She waited until her colour had subsided before she pushed herself up on to her elbows to look at him. 'When you call me Kitten you make me feel ten years old.'

A gleam of devilment entered his eyes while he observed her closely. 'You look ten years old with your hair tied back in a ponytail, and the sea water has washed off your make-up to expose that smattering of freckles on your nose.'

'I don't have freckles on my nose!'

'Oh, yes, you do,' he smiled, bringing his face closer to hers. 'Shall I count them for you?'

'No, thank you!' she said crossly, but she had to look away to hide the smile that quivered on her lips.

'You never told me much about the four years you spent here in Durban at the teacher's training college.' He changed the subject while he rolled over on to his stomach, and she turned her head to see him cup his hands protectively about his lighter when he held the flame to the tip of the cigarette between his lips.

'There wasn't much to tell, and you had objected so strongly to my coming here that I didn't think you would be interested.'

He grimaced. 'I admit that I had fixed ideas about what you would and would not do when you left school, and studying to become a teacher was not one of them.'

Maura stared at him incredulously. 'Did you really think that I would be happy to sit at home and do nothing?'

'I was hoping that you would devote a little of your time to Fieldco,' he explained, frowning down at the smouldering tip of his cigarette.

'I shall always be quite content to leave the business side of Fieldco in your capable hands, and I know I would have become bored to tears devoting only a *little* of my time to the company.' She drew idle patterns in the warm sand with her finger and sighed inwardly at the memory of those terrible arguments they had had in the past because of her decision to become a teacher. 'I needed to do something which would be both stimulating and challenging, and I wanted to do it on my own.'

'I accept that now.' He turned his head and there was a hint of mockery in his smile when he encountered a look of surprise on her face. 'What did you do here at college . . . besides studying, that is?'

'I didn't have much time for all the extramural activities, but I did play tennis when I had a moment to spare,' she explained. 'I wasn't a brilliant scholar, and I had to work hard to pass,' she added defensively when she saw a look of disbelief flash across his handsome, hawk-like features.

'What about boyfriends?'

'There weren't any.'

'Oh, come now, Maura!' He laughed derisively, his strong, white teeth contrasting heavily with his tanned skin, and she could feel her body become heated beneath his critical glance when it trailed over her slender body and lingered for a moment on her firm, shapely bottom. 'You're a very attractive young woman, and there must have been plenty of young men who were clamouring for your attention.'

She looked away and prayed that he would think the sun had put that flush on her cheeks. 'I never lacked an escort when there was a college function I had to attend, but I wasn't very interested in striking up a lasting relationship with any of them.'

'Why not?' Clayton demanded, observing her so intently that she had to look away again.

'Some of them were too immature, and the rest considered themselves so totally irrisistible that they were annoyed when I refused to go to bed with them after the first date.'

'Were you ever tempted to go to bed with any of them?'

Maura's grey glance was indignant. 'You ought to be able to answer that question for yourself.'

Clayton did not answer her at once. He pushed his cigarette stub into the sand, and rolled over on to his side once again to observe her through narrowed eyes.

'I'm not sure that I know the answer,' he said at length, his voice lowered to keep their conversation private when a couple close to them turned their heads to glance at them curiously, but at the same time he seemed to inject a certain intimacy into the atmosphere between them which made Maura's pulses race in alarm. 'You possess a sensuality which tells me that you must, at times, have felt the need for a man to satisfy the cravings of your body.'

Clayton's keen perception seemed to drive the breath from her lungs, and he made her feel embarrassed about something which she had discovered about herself only recently, but it was something which she had not paused to put a name to.

'I had no idea that I possessed such a thing as *sensuality,*' she said in a voice that sounded too husky to be her own, 'and if I have ever felt the need to satisfy any sexual cravings, then I haven't yet succumbed to them.'

His eyes flickered strangely. 'Then you're still a virgin.'

'For God's sake, Clayton!' she hissed, her cheeks flaming and her nerves tangling themselves into knots which she feared might never again become unravelled. 'Could we talk about something else?'

'I thought we were having an intelligent, adult conversation,' Clayton mocked her, his soft, throaty laughter adding to her confusion and embarrassment.

'Well, it's a little too intelligent and adult for me,' she confessed, and he leaned towards her, his warm shoulder brushing against hers as he tilted his head to look into her averted face.

'You look truly delectable when you blush, Kitten,' he teased, and she could not control the burst of nervous laughter which spilled from her lips.

'I think I hate you in this mood,' she said, moving away from his disturbing nearness and sitting up to stare at the bathers surfing out with the waves that crashed towards the shore.

'There's time for a last swim before we return to the hotel for a shower before lunch,' Clayton announced, getting to his feet and towering over her.

His hair lay in a disorderly fashion across his forehead, his skin looked salty, and sand clung to his muscular legs, but it did not diminish that powerful aura of raw maleness he exuded. Dear heaven, it was a sweet agony just to look at him!

'The water is too cold,' she protested.

'That's why I'm suggesting a quick swim,' he said, his smile devilish. 'It will cool you off.'

'I don't need cooling off!' she cried indignantly.

'It doesn't look that way from where I'm standing,' he mocked her, making her blush, and he reached down without warning to take her wrist in a firm, relentless grip. 'Come on, up you get,' he said, the muscles rippling in his arm when he pulled her to her feet and dragged her towards the water's edge.

'Let me go!' she said sharply, embarrassingly aware of people watching them while she struggled helplessly to free her wrist from those steely fingers.

'It seems as if I shall have to help you into the water.'

'Clayton!' she gasped his name, her embarrassment intensifying when he swung her effortlessly into his arms and carried her into the sea. 'Put me down!' she begged, shivering inwardly when she eyed the cold, frothy water swirling beneath her. 'Please, put me down!'

Clayton laughed off her repeated pleas, and he waded deeper into the water until the force of the waves knocked him off his feet. His arms released her when the icy water engulfed them, and she was coughing and gasping for air when at last she surfaced from the boiling bed of the ocean.

Maura wiped the salty water out of her stinging eyes and glared up at him. 'Oh, you—you——'

'Look out!' Clayton's warning cry interrupted her angry retort, and she clutched a little wildly at his shoulders for support when his arm whipped about her waist. She was jerked up against him with a force which almost knocked the breath from her body and, at the same time, she was aware that something hard brushed past against the back of her legs. 'That was close,' he growled angrily. 'Another second or two and that young idiot on his surf board would have careered into you,' he explained, looking down into her startled face. 'Are you all right?'

'Yes, I—I think so,' she stammered, incapable of thinking coherently while his arm still clamped her body so firmly to his hard, muscular frame.

His flesh was cool and damp against hers, but it ignited a pulsing heat inside her, and his mouth was so close to hers that she merely had to raise her face a fraction for their lips to meet.

'I can feel your heart racing,' he murmured, his dark eyes burning down into hers in a way that made her suspect he knew every damning thought that flashed through her mind as well as every shameful desire that clamoured inside her for an outlet.

'I can feel your heart racing too,' she could have said when she became aware of Clayton's heart thudding into her breasts, but she remained silent and a little confused while she assimilated this knowledge. He was not as indifferent to her as he might wish to believe. She could not gauge the extent of his feelings, and she would not dare to assume that they went as deep as her own, but she was very much aware of the fact that her discovery was hampering her attempts to control her wayward emotions. It was the excited shrieks of the bathers around them that finally brought her to her senses.

'Could we go back to the hotel now?' she asked, her hands sliding from his wide shoulders to his hair-roughened chest to ease herself away from those hard hips and muscular thighs, and he released her at once.

'Yes, of course,' he said abruptly, his face an impenetrable mask when he turned from her to surf out with the next wave, and Maura followed suit, praying that the icy water would banish those forbidden thoughts and feelings.

Clayton's manner was distant when they returned to the hotel to shower and change, and Maura was filled with apprehension. She did not want anything to mar these few days in Durban with Clayton, but she discovered later that she had been unnecessarily concerned. He was a perfect companion when they went to the Dolphinarium that afternoon, and she was sufficiently relaxed in his company to enjoy their evening at the theatre. They spent almost the entire Sunday basking in the sun on the beach, and Maura was reluctant to end such a perfect day when they left the hotel restaurant that evening to take the lift up to the seventh floor.

'Do you know what I'd like to do?' She smiled up at Clayton, and he glanced at her enquiringly while they waited for the lift to descend. 'I'd like to go for a walk on the beach,' she explained.

His eyebrows rose a fraction higher. 'We could go for a walk on the promenade, but we're not suitably dressed for a walk on the beach.'

'We could change into something else, couldn't we?'

There was a glimmer of amusement in his eyes when the lift doors slid open to admit them. 'I imagined you would be anxious to have an early night.'

'We don't have to stay out long,' she argued persuasively, and Clayton gestured in agreement before he pressed the required button on the lift's control board.

It was a cool night. She had changed into slacks and a long-sleeved sweater while Clayton wore denims and a blue woollen shirt for their walk, and they found the beach deserted except for a handful of people who had obviously shared Maura's desire to escape the jostling crowds on the promenade. Clayton had rolled up his denims to below his knees, and Maura had done the same with her slacks when they had taken off their shoes to wade in the shallow water.

'It's like walking on the edge of the world.' Maura broke the companionable silence between them. 'On the one side we have the busy foreshore with its festive lights beckoning those who seek entertainment, and on the other side we have the enormous expanse of water which seems to go on forever.' She sighed and paused to stare out across the restless ocean with the luminous waves rushing towards them only to disintegrate about their feet. 'There's nothing out there except the sea, the moon, and the stars.'

'And ships passing in the night,' Clayton added with a hint of mockery in his voice.

'There isn't a ship in sight tonight,' she contradicted

him absently as they continued their walk. 'Do you recall how once we took a drive through the plantation at night?'

'That was a long time ago.'

'I know, but I had the same feeling that night that I was standing on the edge of the world, and that soon, *very* soon, I was going to miss my step and fall.' There was a tightness in her throat and she swallowed convulsively to clear away the constriction. 'My father died a week later.'

'You're in a morbid mood, Kitten,' Clayton rebuked her, taking her hand in his and gripping it firmly. 'What you need is a little strenuous exercise, so let's jog.'

'I didn't come down to the beach to jog, I came to enjoy a quiet walk!' she protested when she found herself dragged along beside him at a running pace.

'Shut up, and jog.'

'This is crazy!' she laughed breathlessly.

'It's healthy,' he countered argumentatively. 'Jogging will get the blood pumping through your veins, and it will clear your head.'

'Who needs a clear head?' she demanded.

Yes, who needs a clear head? she asked herself with cynical amusement. Who needs a clear head on a night like this, on the beach with Clayton, and under circumstances which could prove to be quite romantic?

Good grief! If he could read her thoughts now he would most probably send her straight back to the hotel and up to her room like an errant schoolgirl. This was not a laughing matter, but at that moment she thanked God for her sense of humour, and she began to giggle unrestrainedly.

'You can't laugh and jog at the same time!'

'I—I'm be—beginning to dis—discover that,' she gasped laughingly.

She lost her grip on her sandals, and her legs weakened to the extent that she tripped and stumbled on the cool, uneven sand, but Clayton caught her deftly in his arms before she could land in a crumpled heap at his feet.

'That's what happens when you don't concentrate on what you're doing,' Clayton accused, laughing throatily as he lifted her higher in his arms.

Their laughter mingled as he spun round in a full, dizzying circle, and then, quite suddenly, their laughter faded into a throbbing silence which was disturbed only by the sound of the waves crashing towards the shore.

Maura could feel Clayton's heart beating as hard and fast as her own, and she had the strangest feeling that they had been caught in a trap from which neither of them could find an immediate escape. For one pulsating moment his dark head dipped lower, bringing his face so close to hers that she could feel his warm breath against her mouth, but he did not follow the action through. He had wanted to kiss her, she was convinced of that, but his rigid control had made him check the action before it was too late, and she groaned inwardly when his lips hovered with tantalising uncertainty above hers. It was a dangerous situation for both of them; she had to end it swiftly, but a part of her remained reluctant, and for seemingly endless seconds she fought a silent, futile battle with her conflicting emotions.

Everything inside her had begun to clamour for his kiss and, finally, she found the torment too intolerable to bear. She tightened her arms about his strong neck, and it was she who raised her face that last fractional distance until their lips met in a brief, tentative kiss. Maura drew back slightly, her heart beating in her throat while she waited for him to reject her, but his arms hardened about her, and this time it was Clayton who took the initiative.

Her lips parted beneath his, inviting the intimate invasion of his tongue, and her mind reeled crazily. He had kissed her before, but not with this lingering intent to savour her mouth, and it felt as if he would not stop until he had drawn her heart from her soft, quivering lips. She was faint with ecstasy, and her blood was on fire as it raced through her veins at an intoxicating pace until the sweet agony of desire pulsated through her body.

Her feet were lowered to the sand, but Clayton did not release her. His arms were like steel bands about her, drawing her small softness closer into the hard curve of his aroused body, and she could feel his heart thudding into her breasts when he kissed her with a hungry urgency that seared her to her soul.

The voice of her conscience grew dim, its warning fading into oblivion when Clayton caressed the tender flesh at her waist, and dipped his hand inside the elastic band of her slacks to stroke her bottom. She moaned softly into his plundering mouth, and moved her hips against his in a pagan rhythm of desire which seemed to come to her as naturally as breathing. Her mind had spun out of control, leaving her body in charge, and somehow she found herself lying in Clayton's arms with the cool sand against her back, but she had no recollection of how she had got there. There was only one thing she was conscious of . . . she wanted his touch; she ached for it, and she trembled in exquisite anticipation when his hand shifted up beneath her sweater to stroke the soft swell of her breast.

Maura clung to him on the darkened and deserted stretch of beach. Her fingers tugged at his shirt buttons as her excitement mounted, and her hands revelled in their exploration of his smooth shoulders and his hair-roughened chest. His skin was warm and slightly damp, and he groaned against her mouth when her fingers brushed against his male nipples. She loved him and she wanted him. Oh, God, how she loved him and wanted him!

His hot mouth raked across her throat, his sensual tongue exploring sensitive areas she had not known she possessed, and the sensations he aroused sent shivers of intense pleasure racing through her.

'Oh, Clayton!' she sighed, her voice husky and unfamiliar with passion, but her ecstasy came to an abrupt and shattering end a few moments later when Clayton released her with an angry exclamation on his lips.

He sat up with a jerk, and Maura was momentarily lost and bewildered as she lay there staring at his broad, formidable back. His breathing was as laboured as hers, but that was all that was left of the closeness they had shared. If she raised her hand she could touch him, but it was painfully sobering to know that he had gone beyond her reach mentally, and she wanted to cry out with the agony of it. A shiver raced through her which had nothing to do with the coolness of the night air, and her hands shook uncontrollably when she sat up to pull down her sweater.

Clayton turned his head in the moonlit darkness to look at her, and the silence was ominous and tense until he raked his fingers through his hair in a gesture of agitation. 'Dammit, Maura, I shouldn't have——'

'I know!' she interrupted him hastily, and her unsteady voice was charged with bitterness when she got up to search for the sandals she had dropped on the sand. 'I know you said that it must never happen again, but it *has,* and this time I'm not going to apologise for my part in it.'

She found her sandals as well as Clayton's canvas shoes, and he rose without speaking to take them from her. Her heart felt like lead in her breast when they walked back to the hotel, and she could not look at Clayton in the lift which swept them up to the seventh floor.

'We can't leave things as they are,' he muttered angrily, his hands gripping her shoulders and his fingers biting cruelly into her tender flesh when they stood outside the door to her suite. 'We can't pretend that it never happened, and neither can we pretend that we haven't both been affected by it.'

'I'm not going to pretend anything, Clayton.' She hid her misery behind a shuttered expression when she was forced to meet his dark, stormy glance. 'I wanted you to kiss me, and I wanted you to touch me. What happened between us out there on the beach tonight was something which neither of us could control, and I also happen to know that it's something I shall never want to forget.'

Clayton's mouth tightened in anger. 'I don't think you understand the graveness of the situation.'

'Perhaps not,' she agreed tiredly. 'But I do know how I feel at this moment, and what I feel is something which I know wouldn't interest you in the least.'

'Maura . . .' His fingers bit deeper into her flesh at the sound of approaching footsteps, then he released her to push her roughly into her suite, and closed the door firmly behind them. 'I don't know how *you* feel, Maura, but I'm very much aware of how *I* feel at this moment.' He resumed their conversation in a low, angry growl that sent a stab of fear through her. 'You're a beautiful young woman, and you have proved conclusively that you're capable of making me lose my head. Dammit, don't you *understand?*' he exclaimed harshly, pushing his fingers through his hair in furious agitation. 'I should never have allowed it to happen!'

'There is nothing wrong with what we did.'

'*Everything* is wrong with what we did!' he contradicted her censoriously. 'When you were a child I allowed you to use me as a target on which to practise your wiles and fancies, but that is in the past. You're an adult now, and I dare say you have only just begun to discover the erotic functions of your body, but I'm not going to be used for target practice simply because you think you're safe with me.'

Her face paled, and then the blood rushed back into her cheeks with a stinging force. 'Clayton, I'm not——'

'You have bewitching powers which even I find difficult to resist, Kitten, but that's all it is.' His dark eyes flashed an angry warning which prevented her from interrupting him. 'This has got to stop, Maura, and if you won't do something about it, then I most certainly will!'

'Clayton, will you please *listen* to me?' she begged when he turned from her abruptly.

'We'll meet in the restaurant for breakfast at eight sharp in the morning,' he said, ignoring her plea and casting a stern glance over his wide shoulder as he opened the door. 'And don't be late!'

Maura stood staring at the door for a long time after he had gone, then she turned away with a shuddering sigh. She had said that she was not going to pretend, but, for the sake of her own sanity, she knew that she would have to pretend that nothing had happened. She showered, washed the sand out of her hair, and put on her nightgown, but she carried out this nightly ritual like an automaton, rigidly banning thoughts of Clayton from her mind. It took a considerable time before she was ready to get into bed, but her mind would no longer be still when she slid between the cool sheets and switched off the light.

Over and over, like a recurring nightmare, her mind replayed that forbidden incident on the beach. She could still feel his warm hands stroking her body, and the heat of his mouth against her skin. He had awakened her to sensations and emotions which she had never encountered before, and even now the memory of it aroused an aching tightness in her loins which made her groan and turn her hot face into the cool pillow to seek escape from her thoughts, but her mind was relentless.

Clayton had not attempted to absolve himself from what had occurred between them, and that was something she ought to be grateful for. He might persist in thinking of her as his sister, but he had not treated her like his sister on the beach. He had wanted her as a man wants a woman he is attracted to physically. This was something which ought to have filled her with elation, but instead it made her plunge deeper into that pit of misery she had dug for herself by falling in love with Clayton. She wanted more from him than the mere knowledge that he was physically attracted to her. She wanted his love, the love a man has for the woman he wants to spend the rest of his life with, but she was beginning to have grave doubts about ever getting what she wanted.

I'm not going to be used for target practice simply because you think you're safe with me! Everything else seemed to pale into insignificance beside that revealing remark. How was she ever going to make him believe that she really loved him?

Maura did not sleep very well, but during the past months she had become accustomed to lying awake at night. She had never imagined that loving someone could cause such anxiety and tension, but, then, she had never imagined that she would fall in love with a man who was so stoically concerned with the fact that he was her stepbrother.

Clayton was polite but distant during the course of the business they had to attend to, and he involved her so completely that she barely had time to think about anything else. On the Tuesday morning, just before lunch, their purchases were finalised, and the agreement signed. The new machinery and equipment required for the expansions to the mill would be delivered during the third week in August, and it would be erected on the site at Fieldco.

Maura had learnt a considerable amount about the business side of Fieldco during those two days, and her admiration and respect for Clayton had grown. He had a brilliant and alert mind. He needed quality in the goods which he purchased at an exorbitant price, and nothing escaped his notice, not even the slightest suggestion of a flaw. The legal loopholes in the agreement did not go unnoticed either, and the young sales manager was visibly relieved and suitably in awe of Clayton when they finally attached their signatures to the document which had, at last, been drawn up to Clayton's satisfaction.

Maura was mentally exhausted when they drove back to the hotel, and she made no attempt at polite conversation. When Clayton's hand accidentally brushed against her knee while he was changing gear, he muttered an apology, and Maura might have laughed out loud if it had not been for that aching tightness which had a stranglehold on her throat. He had gone to great lengths during the past two days to avoid physical contact between them, and that tightness in her throat brought a sudden rush of tears to her eyes when she recalled how, in the crowded hotel lift that morning, he had hastily shifted his position when his arm had touched hers.

Oh, dear God in heaven! Did he have to treat her as if she had suddenly become leprous? If only she could laugh it all off instead of letting it hurt so much. If only . . .!

She turned her head away, blinking back the tears before Clayton saw them, and she focused her attention on the midday Durban traffic as if it were she who was behind the wheel instead of Clayton. She was not going to fall to pieces simply because she had given her love where it was not wanted! *Love is a state of mind,* someone had once told her, and she had enough strength left to control her mind before her mind controlled *her!*

She was not very hungry when they sat down to lunch that day, but it was obvious that Clayton was famished. He waded through his steak and salads as if he had not a care in the world, but Maura merely rearranged the food on her plate, and she could almost hate him for looking so unperturbed.

'We'll leave for home after breakfast tomorrow morning,' he said when they were drinking their tea. 'Did you perhaps want to visit your aunt this afternoon?'

'I'm rather tired,' she told him, staring fixedly into the cup of tea in front of her. 'I think I would prefer to spend the afternoon resting in my suite.'

'You won't mind, then, if I visit a few business acquaintances of mine while I still have the chance to catch them at their offices?'

'I shan't mind at all.'

In her suite, half an hour later, Maura took a cool, refreshing shower, and she stood for a long time enjoying the almost therapeutic pelting of the water on her body before she dried herself and slipped into her long-sleeved silk robe for comfort. She lay down on her bed, but she did not intend to sleep. She simply wanted to relax, but, after a few minutes, her eyelids started to droop, and she did not resist when she felt herself drifting hazily into that blessed state of oblivion which had been so elusive the past two nights.

She slept deeply, but even in her dreams she was tormented, and it was with a feeling of relief that she awakened several hours later to find her room almost in darkness. This was their last night in Durban, and she was glad that they were going home tomorrow.

CHAPTER NINE

THE weather was scorchingly hot on the Wednesday morning when they left Durban and headed north on the N3 towards New Ansbach, but the temperature remained comfortably cool during the four-hour journey in Clayton's air-conditioned Jaguar. Maura was silent most of the way, and neither did Clayton encourage conversation. There was, after all, nothing to say which they had not said to each other before, but the discomfiting silence between them was eased considerably when Clayton slipped a cassette into the car radio. The first strains of a Beethoven symphony fell gently on Maura's ears, and she closed her eyes, willing herself to relax as she put her head back against the headrest.

She wished that she could forget that it was Clayton who was sitting beside her, but that was impossible. She felt his presence as strongly as she felt her own heart beating in her breast, and she could almost hate him for his relaxed but alert appearance behind the wheel. How could he look so calm while her emotions were in such a painful turmoil?

It was after midday when they caught their first glimpse of New Ansbach. The Lutheran church spire and the clock-tower of the town hall jutted out above the trees, and it had never been a more welcome sight. They would soon be home, and then, hopefully, some of the tension would ease between them.

Ten minutes later Clayton parked his Jaguar in the driveway below the shallow steps leading up to Hilltop

House's pillared entrance, and Maura was easing her stiff body out of the car when Angela Fielding emerged from the house, but Angela was not alone. A tall, attractive brunette was hurrying down to the car ahead of Angela, her high heels clicking on the slate steps, and she brushed past Maura without so much as a glance to fling herself into Clayton's waiting arms.

'Clayton!' she exclaimed in a husky voice, her arms locked about his neck as she kissed and embraced him in a way which suggested an intimate familiarity between them, and Maura was aware of a new kind of pain which she did not pause to analyse. 'Darling, I'm so glad you're back!'

Darling? Maura stiffened with displeasure. Who was this woman, and what was she doing here?

'This is a pleasant surprise, Val,' Clayton responded, smiling warmly down into those violet-blue eyes raised to his, and he had made no attempt to extricate himself from those pale, slender arms when Maura turned, rigid-faced, to greet her stepmother.

'I telephoned the office and, when your secretary told me that you were expected back this morning, I thought I'd drop by to welcome you home,' the brunette explained coyly. 'Your mother has invited me to stay to lunch. I hope you don't mind, darling?'

'I'm delighted!'

'And this must be your sister.' The woman smiled as she turned in the circle of Clayton's arm to face Maura who was standing stiff and silent beside Angela.

'Yes.' Clayton's smile faded, and the coolness that entered his eyes sent an icy sensation spiralling through Maura. 'Maura, I'd like you to meet Valerie Austen.'

'How do you do, Miss Austen,' Maura murmured politely, hiding her feelings behind an outwardly calm expression.

'Oh, call me Val. Everybody does.' Valerie Austen stressed this with a casual wave of a slender, manicured hand, and she dismissed Maura at the same time to focus her attention on Clayton once again. 'Darling, I've missed you dreadfully.'

'And I've missed you,' Clayton replied, lowering his dark head to Val's to kiss her crimson, pouting lips, and Maura looked away when yet another stab of pain tore through her.

'Shall we go inside?' Angela intervened, linking her arm through Maura's. 'There's time for something cool to drink before we sit down to lunch.'

The agony of the ensuing hour was something which Maura did not want to live through again. Valerie Austen was not someone whom one could overlook or ignore. She was clever, charming, sophisticated and witty, and Clayton's hawk-like features bore the look of a man who was totally captivated. Their eyes met often across the table, speaking an intimate language which excluded Maura and Angela, and Maura's hopes and dreams withered and died like a flower which had been left without water in the blazing summer sun.

Clayton telephoned Mrs Thompson, his secretary, to ask her to postpone his appointments for the afternoon, and Maura was actually relieved when Clayton and Valerie Austen excused themselves and left in Valerie's Nissan Exa.

The silence in the dining-room was so heavy it was almost tangible after their departure and, despite the amount of sugar Maura had spooned into her cup, every mouthful of tea tasted like gall.

'How long has Clayton known Valerie Austen?' Maura questioned her stepmother when she could no longer contain her curiosity.

Angela looked thoughtful as she helped herself to a

second cup of tea. 'I think they met each other about two years ago at the home of a business associate in Vryheid, and since then they have been seeing each other quite regularly.'

'Why has no one ever mentioned her name in my presence?'

'I really can't say,' Angela replied, the look of surprise on her face lending authenticity to her statement.

'She knows her way around Hilltop House, so she has obviously been here before.'

'She has been here several times,' Angela confirmed, 'but somehow her visits never coincided with yours.'

Only one question remained to be asked, and Maura steeled herself mentally to receive the answer. 'Is Clayton going to marry her?'

'I have no idea, but I should imagine that their relationship wouldn't have lasted this long if he wasn't serious about her.' Angela observed Maura curiously while she put down her cup and dabbed at her mouth with her table napkin. 'Why do you want to know if he's going to marry her?'

'Oh . . . no reason.'

Maura's outwardly casual appearance belied the pain inside her as she rose to her feet and crossed the room to stare out of the window with unseeing eyes.

'You're in love with Clayton, Maura.' It was a statement, not a query, and it felt as if the air had been sucked from Maura's lungs as she spun round nervously to find her stepmother observing her with a tender, understanding warmth in her eyes. 'Oh, don't look so stricken, my dear. I've suspected for some time now that your feelings for my son had changed into something deeper, and I might as well admit that it has always been my dearest wish that the two of you would marry each other some day. Clayton, of course, is like his father: a closed book until he himself chooses to reveal his feelings.'

'Oh, Mother!' she groaned, close to tears as she returned to her chair at the table and sat down heavily. 'I've been doing nothing these past months but hope and pray that I could break through that barrier he has erected between us, and I was beginning to think that I stood a chance, but . . . ' She stared down at her clenched hands in her lap, and shook her head dismally. 'Not any more.'

'Valerie Austen.' Angela murmured the name quietly, and with compassionate understanding, but it fell like the blow of an axe on Maura's heart, drawing blood. 'I must confess, my dear, that I am only assuming that their relationship is serious.'

'She's very beautiful and sophisticated, and . . . ' Maura swallowed convulsively at the memory of the warmth in Clayton's eyes whenever he had looked at Valerie, and there was a fierceness in her tear-filled glance when she raised her head proudly to look at her stepmother. 'If he marries Valerie Austen, then she had better make him happy, or I'll—I'll scratch her eyes out!'

To Maura's horror, she burst into near-hysterical tears in front of her astonished stepmother, and she fled from the dining-room in a blind haste to reach her bedroom where she wept as she had not wept since the day her father died.

The third term at school started with a vengeance, but Maura did not object. She was kept busy, too busy really to have time to think about herself, and she preferred it that way. She stayed in town weekends, and joined the New Ansbach tennis club as an excuse not to go home to Hilltop House. She was fighting a bitter and fierce battle to overcome her feelings for Clayton, and the less she saw of him, the better for her. Angela came to town quite frequently, and she often arrived at the cottage to enjoy a quick cup of tea with Maura and Joan before returning home.

'I haven't wanted to pry,' Joan remarked one afternoon after Angela had left, 'but you looked like death when you returned from your holiday. You've been working yourself to a frenzy ever since, and you haven't been home once since the term started. May I know what is wrong?'

Maura collected their empty cups and placed them in the tray. 'I have found that work is the best antidote when you love someone who happens to be in love with someone else.'

'Clayton is in love with someone else?' Joan followed Maura into the kitchen with a look of disbelief on her face.

'Yes,' Maura confirmed, placing the cups in the sink, and emptying out the teapot. 'Her name is Valerie Austen, and he has known her for two years.'

'That doesn't mean he's going to *marry* her!'

'To quote my stepmother, their relationship wouldn't have lasted for two years if he wasn't serious about her.' Maura smiled twistedly and added a squirt of detergent to the water she was running into the sink. 'And you didn't see them together the way I did.'

The memory of that day, when they had returned from Durban to find Valerie Austen waiting at Hilltop House, was branded as if with fire into Maura's brain, and the pain of it was something she had not yet been capable of shedding.

'I'm sorry.'

'I'm the one who is sorry!' Maura laughed bitterly, turning off the taps and dipping her hands into the sudsy water to wash the cups with an unnecessary vigour. 'A one-sided love doesn't stand a chance, and I'll get over it even if it kills me!' she added, gritting her teeth with a fierce determination.

The subject was not mentioned again between them, and during the ensuing weeks Maura fought her solitary battle to the point where she could almost say with confidence that she had overcome her feelings for Clayton. There was still that twinge of envy whenever she heard Joan and Will discussing the plans for their December wedding, but that, too, was fading. She had not seen Clayton since the new school term had started. Their first communication had been a brief note from Clayton which he had attached to Fieldco's month-end report to draw her attention to something which he had particularly wanted her to take note of. The second letter had been hastily written on his small desk pad.

'Mother is missing you,' he had written in his bold handwriting. 'Surely you're not too busy to spend at least one weekend at home?'

Mother is missing you! Clayton could have said, *'We are missing you'*. It would have been polite, if nothing else, but . . .! Oh, *hell,* it shouldn't matter, but it *did!* It hurt! She had thought that she had conquered her feelings, but Clayton's coldness towards her still had the diabolical power to hurt her.

'I shall have to disappoint Mother a while longer, but I'm sure she'll understand,' Maura had replied with an equally brief note to which she had received no response.

They were well into spring, and midway through the end of term exams, when Maura awoke one morning with a strange feeling of anxiety clutching at her chest. She was not prone to premonitions, and she tried to shake it off during the course of the morning, but it remained with her like a second shadow. It made her nervous and edgy, and she jumped visibly when the Principal's voice crackled over the intercom during the final period of that day to announce the total of the funds which had been raised with the spring walk.

Maura shivered and calmed herself, but when she drove away from the school that afternoon, her hands were clenched so tightly around the steering-wheel that her fingers were aching when she arrived at the cottage.

'What's the matter with you today?' Joan teased when they had made themselves a cup of tea. 'You look as if you're expecting to meet a ghost, but you're not sure when.'

'Oh, I don't really know.' She stirred her tea agitatedly and dropped her teaspoon into the saucer with a clatter. 'For some obscure reason I have this crazy feeling that something dreadful is going to happen, and it has haunted me since the moment I opened my eyes this morning.'

'You've been working much too hard, that's the problem.'

'I hope you're right.' Maura smiled self-consciously, praying that Joan was right, but she could not shake off her uneasiness.

They were still drinking their tea in the kitchen when the telephone rang shrilly in the lounge, and Maura froze in her chair, an icy sensation spiralling through her.

'I'll get it.' Joan's eyes sparkled with amusement when she rose from her chair and walked briskly out of the kitchen. The silence was almost deafening when the ringing stopped. Maura could hear a brief mumble of meaningless words, and a few seconds later a grave-looking Joan returned to the kitchen. 'It's your mother, and she sounds as if she's upset about something.'

I knew it! The words screamed through Maura's brain like a wailing siren as she leapt to her feet and stormed out of the kitchen. *I knew something dreadful was going to happen today!*

'What's wrong, Mother?' she demanded anxiously when she had snatched up the receiver.

'It's Clayton.' Angela's voice was choked with anxiety and suppressed tears. 'A stack of lumber collapsed. I don't know all the details about the accident, but he was rushed to the Vryheid hospital in a critical condition.'

'Oh, God!' Fear, cold and sickening, surged through her as the room started to spin around her, and she sat down heavily on the chair beside the telephone when a dreaded blackness threatened to engulf her. She had never fainted in her life before, and she could not afford to faint now, she told herself fiercely. 'Where are you calling from, Mother?' she asked when she had succeeded in pulling herself together to some extent.

'I'm here at the Vryheid hospital.' Angela's voice was still wavery, but it gained strength as she continued. 'I arranged with Fieldco's chauffeur to drive me through, but I sent the car back. I'm not leaving this hospital until I know the full extent of Clayton's injuries.'

Maura did not need time to deliberate her actions. 'I'm leaving New Ansbach immediately,' she told her stepmother, 'and I'll be at the hospital as soon as my car can make it to Vryheid.'

She was tight-lipped and ashen-faced, and her hand was shaking to such an extent that she had difficulty in placing the receiver on its cradle.

'What has happened?' Joan demanded.

'There was an accident in the lumber yard, and Clayton was rushed to the Vryheid hospital,' Maura explained without pausing in her mad dash to collect her handbag and car keys where she had left them in the bedroom. 'I don't know when I'll be back,' she added when Joan followed her out of the cottage. 'I intend to stay as long as I'm needed, but I'll keep in touch.'

Vryheid was thirty minutes away from New Ansbach, but on that afternoon it seemed to take hours, and Maura dared not push her Volkswagen harder that its protesting engine would allow. Oh, what would she not have given at that moment to have had the speed of that Mercedes which Clayton had wanted her to buy some months ago!

She did not dare speculate about the severity of Clayton's injuries. Not being in possession of the facts merely intensified her anxiety, and . . .! Oh, God, please don't let him die!

Maura found Angela pacing the floor in a small, sparsely furnished waiting-room. Her stepmother pressed a handkerchief to her quivering mouth, and she collapsed tearfully into Maura's arms the moment she saw her. Maura's throat tightened with tears and her eyes stung, but she did not let her rigid control slip. She had to be strong for Angela's sake. There would be time for tears later, but not now when Angela needed someone to lean on.

'I'm so glad you're here,' Angela sighed shakily when they drew apart. 'I don't think I could have tolerated being alone in this dismal room for a moment longer.'

'Have you heard anything more since we spoke on the phone?'

Angela dabbed ineffectively at her tear-filled eyes with her lacy handkerchief and shook her head. 'All I know is that Clayton is being X-rayed at this moment to determine the extent of his injuries, but beyond that everyone is so vague that I could scream.'

The antiseptic smell of the hospital quivered in Maura's nostrils, and her glance darted about the room to settle on the tray of tea which stood untouched on the low, circular table between two upright chairs. 'Is that tea fresh?'

Angela nodded, her face pale and haggard, and Maura poured a cup, adding milk and sugar as she knew her stepmother liked it.

'Sit down, and drink this cup of tea,' she instructed

quietly, placing the cup in Angela's hands, and urging her on to one of the upright chairs against the wall.

Angela raised the cup to her lips with a hand that trembled, but she paused half-way in the action, and there was naked fear in her eyes. 'Oh, Maura, what if——'

'*No!*' Maura's voice was sharp—for her stepmother's sake as well as her own. 'Almost from the moment I received your call I have been telling myself not to speculate about Clayton's injuries until I know the facts, and I suggest you do the same.'

'You're right, of course.' Angela attempted a smile, but it went awry, and renewed tears filled those dark eyes which reminded Maura so much of Clayton that she wanted to cry out with the agony of it. 'It's silly of me to fall apart like this, but I—I really don't know what I'm going to do if anything happens to my son.'

'Drink your tea before it's cold,' Maura suggested with a calmness she was not experiencing at that moment, and she looked away to hide the evidence of her own tears. Any icy dread seemed to be drawing every vestige of warmth from her face and her body to leave her chilled to the marrow. Dear God . . . *please!* Life without Clayton was unthinkable!

The minutes continued to drag like hours, and that small waiting-room felt like a prison while they waited anxiously for news. They sat in silence, holding hands at times, and too afraid to voice their terrified thoughts, but they each found a certain comfort in the presence of the other.

Maura's nerves were becoming horribly frayed, and she was not sure how much longer she could bear the uncertainty. She was tempted to go in search of someone in authority who could give them an indication as to what was going on, but she knew the futility of such an action. Only the doctor could give them the information they wanted, and he could only do that after a lengthy, thorough examination.

An eternity seemed to pass with nurses walking back and forth at a brisk pace along the passage, but Maura and Angela exchanged an anxious glance at the sound of unmistakably male footsteps approaching the waiting-room, and they rose hastily to their feet when a man in a white hospital jacket walked into the room.

His glance skipped over Maura and settled with recognition on Angela. 'Good afternoon, Mrs Fielding.'

'How is my son, Dr Rennie?' she questioned him directly and without preamble, and Maura's heart took a frightened leap into her throat at the tight-lipped gravity of the elderly doctor's expression.

'He is severely concussed, and he has three cracked ribs, but the injury which conerens us most is the heavy blow he received on his spine,' he explained in that calm, detached manner practised by people in the medical profession. 'We can't determine the extent of the spinal injury while he is still unconscious, but the X-rays show a definite contusion.'

'You mean he might be paralysed?' Angela voiced the terrifying query which had leapt into Maura's own mind.

'I didn't say that, Mrs Fielding,' he said hastily, the first hint of a smile invading the sternness of his expression. 'The spinal cord isn't severed, so we have no reason to diagnose a permanent paralysis, but we have called in a neuro-surgeon, and we should have more definite news for you within the next couple of hours.'

Angela was pale, but perfectly controlled now as she faced Dr Rennie. 'May I see my son?'

'Of course you may.' He smiled again. 'Come with me.'

'May I see him as well?' Maura spoke for the first time and, when the doctor hesitated, Angela linked her arm through Maura's.

'This is my stepdaughter, Maura Fielding,' she said, and Dr Rennie nodded, his expression clearing as he led the way out of the cramped waiting-room.

They followed him in silence down several passages, their footsteps echoing hollowly on the tiled floor, and Maura steeled herself mentally when the doctor paused to push open a door which had stood ajar. He stood aside for them to precede him into the clinical ward, and they filed past him in silence, scarcely noticing the nurse who had risen respectfully beside the high hospital bed.

Tears stung Maura's eyelids when she stood looking down at Clayton. His face was unnaturally pale, and they had shaved off his hair behind his right ear to insert stitches in a six-centimetre-long gash. He was lying flat on his back without a pillow beneath his head, and Maura's heart lurched violently in her breast. Oh, if only he would open his eyes, or move a finger so that she could be sure that he was still alive, but instead he was lying there so quietly beneath the stark white bedclothes that she found herself searching frantically for a visible sign that he was still breathing.

'Dear God, he's so pale and still that one could almost believe he is dead,' Angela whispered in distress, her words echoing Maura's own alarming thoughts.

'Oh, he's very much alive.' The young nurse smiled at them reassuringly across Clayton's prone figure on the bed. 'And, if you don't mind my saying so, he's quite the handsomest patient I've had to attend to in my two years of training.'

She had meant well, but her remark had obviously evoked Dr Rennie's displeasure. He frowned at her and said abruptly, 'That will be all for the moment, Nurse.'

'Yes, Doctor,' she replied soberly.

Dr Rennie turned to Angela when the nurse had left the

ward. 'Mrs Fielding, I would like to suggest that you go home instead of waiting around here in the hospital,' he said. 'I'll call you as soon we have definite news about your son's condition, but for the moment there is nothing anyone can do except keep him as quiet and as comfortable as possible until the neuro-surgeon is free to see him.'

'And when will that be?' Angela demanded quietly, her head bowed as she covered Clayton's lifeless hand with her own.

'Not for another hour or more.'

Angela did not respond to Dr Rennie's suggestion that they go home. Her grim face registered a certain reluctance, and it was Maura who made the decision.

'We'll wait,' she told the doctor, and there was an unexpected look of approval in Angela's dark eyes when Maura glanced at her.

'Please yourselves,' the doctor shrugged resignedly, gesturing towards the door to indicate that their brief visit to his comatose patient was at an end. 'If you want something to eat or drink then you have only to ask one of the nurses on duty.'

'Thank you, Doctor,' they murmured almost in unison as they preceded him out of the ward and made their own silent way back to the waiting-room.

Maura made two telephone calls. One was to Joan to let her know what was happening, and the other was to the staff at Hilltop House. There was nothing to do after that except to wait, but Mrs Thompson, Clayton's secretary, caused a brief diversion when she arrived at the hospital shortly before six that evening. She did not linger unnecessarily after they had informed her of Clayton's condition, and their seemingly endless wait continued.

It was dark outside, and the electric light hanging from the high ceiling did nothing to ease the antiseptic atmosphere of the hospital waiting-room. It was approaching seven o'clock when the young nurse they had met at Clayton's bedside brought them a tray of tea and sandwiches. She also delivered the welcome news that the neuro-surgeon had arrived, and that he was, at that moment, carrying out his examination.

Their long, agonising wait was now almost at an end, but Maura hovered somewhere between relief and a terrible anxiety. Would the neuro-surgeon's examination reveal what they prayed it would, or was it going to condemn Clayton to a future which would have to be spent in a wheelchair?

Oh, God! Not that! Please don't make a helpless invalid out of someone who has always been so active and so vitally alive! Please, God!

Maura's glance met Angela's and she saw in those dark eyes the same fears which were tearing her apart inside. Gunther Brauer had died in a similar accident almost thirty years before, and now his son's fate was still hanging in the balance. Clayton's life had been spared, that was something to be grateful for. But what kind of life would he have as a helpless cripple?

'Let's eat,' Maura announced firmly, shutting her mind to her fears as she got up to pour their tea.

'I'm not really hungry,' Angela protested when Maura passed her the plate, but she helped herself reluctantly to a ham and egg sandwich.

'Neither am I,' Maura confessed, 'but we're liable to collapse under the strain if we don't eat something.'

'I don't know what I would have done without you, Maura. You're so calm and so strong in this moment of crisis that I'm ashamed of myself.'

Calm and strong? A wave of hysteria rose up inside Maura, but she quelled it forcibly and helped herself to a sandwich. She was not calm and strong. She was a bundle of nervous anxiety, and she was scared out of her wits.

They had not been very hungry, but they emptied the plate of sandwiches between them, and helped themselves to a second cup of tea. Maura could not recall the taste of the sandwiches. Eating and drinking their tea had given them something to do to alleviate the stress and the strain of waiting, but the tension rose steadily to an unbearable level during those final, seemingly endless minutes before they would know the verdict, and Maura had to force herself not to get up and pace the floor alongside Angela.

Maura's ears had become attuned to the hum of activity in the hospital. Every clink of metal upon metal, every squeak of a trolley, and every brisk footstep on the tiled floor was jarring her nerves and making her heart beat in a wild, panic-stricken tattoo against her ribs. She was shaking inwardly, and she was clenching her jaw so tightly that her face was aching when Dr Rennie finally put in an appearance.

'I have promising news.' He smiled at them, and Maura's heart leapt in nervous anticipation. 'The injury to Mr Brauer's spine is not as serious as we initially thought. It will require treatment and two weeks of lying flat on his back, but at the same time I don't wish to minimise the gravity of his present condition. He is still unconscious, and if his comatose condition lingers on it could hamper his recovery.'

Those icy fingers of fear and anxiety were sliding resolutely about Maura's heart again, and she could feel the coldness surging into her body.

'Are you expecting complications?' Angela asked that dreaded question.

'Complications *could* set in,' Dr Rennie admitted gravely. 'At the moment we have no reason not to expect a complete recovery, but the human body is unpredictable, and we cannot entirely rule out the possibity of complications.'

Angela dabbed unashamedly at the moisture in her eyes, then she squared her shoulders. 'I thank you for your honesty, Dr Rennie, and I shall go home now, but I would like to see my son again for a few minutes before I leave.'

Dr Rennie nodded agreeably, but this time Maura chose not to accompany her stepmother to Clayton's ward. She could not bear to be near him while her mind and her heart were in such an emotional turmoil. Her veneer of calmness was beginning to crack and, if it crumbled completely, she would burst into tears.

The drive from the hospital to New Ansbach that evening was equally endless. Maura could think of nothing to say, and neither, it seemed, could Angela. They stopped at the cottage for Maura to collect her briefcase and a few items of clothing. She had decided to spend the night with Angela at Hilltop House, and Joan agreed that it would be wise not to leave her stepmother alone after the hours of anxiety they had endured together.

Angela was reluctant to go to bed that night, and so was Maura. They found a pot of soup simmering on the stove in the kitchen, and they helped themselves to a bowl of steaming vegetable broth. The telephone rang several times, tearing at Maura's fragile nerves, but the calls were merely from Fieldco employees who were concerned about Clayton.

Maura was exhausted in mind and body when they eventually went to bed, but she could not sleep. She could not shut out the memory of Clayton's tall, muscular frame lying so inert on that high hospital bed, and she could not ignore that gnawing fear that something might happen to impede his recovery. She wished that she could cry to relieve the tension inside her, but the tears would not come, and she spent a fretful night tossing about in her bed.

She was up and dressed at five the following morning to call the hospital to enquire about Clayton and to seek their permission to see him before she went to the school. Angela was standing beside her when she replaced the receiver, the ravages of a sleepless night as clearly evident on her face as they were on Maura's, and they embraced each other silently in a mutual desire for comfort.

'I'm going to the hospital before school starts this morning,' Maura informed her stepmother. 'Call me if there's a change in his condition, and I'll arrange for someone else to take my classes.'

Angela nodded without speaking, and Maura left a few minutes later, pushing her Volkswagen to its limit once again on the road to Vryheid.

Maura was grey-faced and tired when she walked into Clayton's ward and, no matter how cleverly she had applied her make-up, she had been incapable of disguising the shadows beneath her troubled eyes. The nurse on duty was not the one they had met the night before, but her smile was equally friendly when she vacated her chair and left the ward to give Maura a few minutes alone with Clayton.

He had not moved, it seemed, since the last time she had seen him, but there appeared to be a suggestion of colour in his lean, unshaven cheeks. A bottle of colourless fluid hung from a metal stand beside his bed, and it released a steady flow of drops into a tube which looped down to his arm. They were feeding him intravenously, that much she knew, but it did not allay her fears.

She lowered herself on to the chair beside his bed and her heart was beating painfully in her throat when she took his sun-browned hand between her own. She had never seen him look so vulnerable and so helpless, and everything inside her revolted against it.

'Oh, Clayton!' Tears stung her eyes and spilled from her lashes as she pressed her quivering lips to the back of his hand and rested her cheek against it. 'You have to get better! You just *have* to, do you hear me?'

She raised her head to look at him, to will him back, if she could, from wherever he had drifted to, but his face remained a motionless blur through her tears.

'I love you, Clayton, and you have to get better because, you see, I need you even if you don't need me,' she whispered, speaking her anguished thoughts aloud almost without realising it. 'Don't be angry with me, Clayton. I didn't want to fall in love with you, and I tried my best not to, but I simply couldn't help it. I guess I've always loved you, and I know I always will.'

It was a relief to cry at last, and she was weeping silently with Clayton's hand still held firmly between her own when someone touched her shoulder.

'Are you all right, Miss Fielding?'

Maura sat up with a start to find the nurse standing beside her, and she smiled a little self-consciously. 'Yes,' she sniffed, searching her handbag for her elusive handkerchief. 'Yes, I'm fine, thank you.'

'I'm afraid I have to ask you to leave now.'

Maura nodded and rose from the chair, but her glance sharpened when she released Clayton's hand. She could not swear to it, but it had looked as if he had moved his fingers slightly. No, she must have imagined it, she told herself when there was no further sign of movement, and she leaned over him quickly to brush her lips gently against his forehead.

'I'll come again this afternoon, Clayton,' she promised in a whisper as if he could hear her.

CHAPTER TEN

MAURA received a telephone call from Angela that morning. It came shortly after eleven o'clock when Angela had known that Maura would be having tea in the staff-room, and Maura had shed tears of relief when she had heard Angela's heart-warming news. Clayton had regained consciousness that morning, and Dr Rennie, acting in accordance with the neuro-surgeon's instructions, had prescribed complete rest for the first few days. He would be allowed one visitor twice daily for a brief period only, and it was agreed that Angela would visit Clayton in the mornings, while Maura would restrict her visits to the afternoons.

Clayton was sleeping naturally that first afternoon when Maura arrived at the hospital, and she stayed beside his bed only a few minutes. They talked a little on the second day before he dropped off to sleep again, but on the third day he was wide awake and demanding to know when he could leave the hospital.

'Don't be impatient, Clayton, and don't do anything which might jeopardise your recovery,' Maura reasoned with him, and she was thinking in particular about his spinal injury. 'You're really very lucky to be alive.'

'I realise that.' His hand moved against the white coverlet, and she clasped it between her own, not caring what he might think. 'It was good of you to come, Maura, and I must thank you for staying at home with Mother that first night.'

'You don't have to thank me, Clayton.' Her voice

169

cracked with emotion at the memory of the nightmare
they had lived through during those anxious hours while
they had waited for news. 'We were both extremely
worried about you.'

'Were you really worried, Kitten?'

'Yes, I was,' she confessed unsteadily, her grey eyes
clouding with remembered fear as she sustained his
searching glance. 'I was terrified at the thought that you
might die.'

His fingers tightened about hers, and there was
something in his eyes that made her heart leap wildly in
her breast, but it was gone the next instant when the
sound of approaching footsteps made them glance
towards the door which stood ajar. A stern-faced nursing
sister entered the ward, and Maura knew that this
heralded the end of her visit.

'I must ask you to leave now, Miss Fielding,' she
announced in a voice which was as brisk as her manner.
'Mr Brauer needs plenty of rest.'

'I'll come again tomorrow,' Maura promised Clayton,
releasing his hand, and she left hurriedly before the stern-
faced woman found it necessary to repeat her authoritative command.

Maura was in a buoyant mood when she arrived back
at the cottage that afternoon, and Joan was quick to
notice the change when she followed Maura into her
bedroom.

'I gather that Clayton's recuperation is satisfactory?'

'Oh, yes!' Maura sighed happily, dumping her
briefcase on the floor at the front of her bed, and kicking
off her shoes. 'He still feels a bit bruised and battered,
but he's going to get well, and I can't tell you what a
tremendous relief it is to know that.'

'And what about you? Joan demanded curiously.
'How is this going to affect your recovery.'

Maura frowned. 'What do you mean?'

'You're still in love with him.'

Maura winced inwardly and looked away to hide the naked pain in her eyes. 'You once told me that no one could switch their feelings on or off at will, and that they have to run their natural course, either to fade or grow into something strong and permanent.'

'And yours have grown strong and permanent?' Joan added in a quiet, sympathetic voice.

'I'm afraid so.' Maura sighed heavily to ease that tightness in her chest, and she raised her hands in a gesture of despair. 'It's something I shall simply have to learn to live with.'

'I wish I could do something to help.'

'There is nothing anyone can do.' Maura pulled herself together with an effort and she forced her stiff lips into a smile as she turned to face Joan. 'Is it my turn to prepare the dinner?'

'Joan pulled a face. 'No, it's my turn tonight.'

'In that case,' Maura laughed at her, 'I'll have a quick bath and start correcting that massive pile of exam papers I brought home with me.'

'Don't remind me about the pile of work I still have to get through,' Joan groaned as she wandered off into the kitchen to start their dinner.

Maura made no attempt to deny to herself that she was bursting with impatience to see Clayton again. She practically wished away the hours, but she was quite unprepared for what she encountered when she entered his ward the following afternoon. Valerie Austen was there. She was sitting beside his bed, and it was a sobering shock to see them holding hands and talking softly like lovers.

'You're so fortunate, Maura,' Valerie announced, pouting her crimson mouth and looking petulant. 'I was told that only the family was allowed to visit Clayton, and they wouldn't let me in until this afternoon.'

Maura could have given the attractive brunette one very good reason why she did not consider it fortunate to be classified as family, but she remained silent, and forced her stiff lips into a semblance of a smile.

'Darling,' Val purred like a satisfied kitten, her attention focused on Clayton. 'If there's anything you would like me to get for you, then you only have to say so.'

'All I need is for you to bring yourself,' he smiled warmly.

'You don't even need to ask, darling,' Val murmured with a note of intimacy in her husky voice. 'From now on you're going to see me every afternoon and evening when visitors are allowed.'

Maura felt as if she had intruded where she did not belong, and she recognised that searing stab of pain for what it was. She was jealous! She despised herself for it, but . . . oh, God, how she wished that she could be sharing that easy intimacy with Clayton.

Afraid that her feelings might show, she glanced at her watch, and made a pretence of being rushed for time. 'I hope you'll forgive me, but I must leave now.'

'So soon?' Valerie demanded, but her look of disappointment lacked sincerity.

'The children are writing their end-of-term exams, and I have a pile of papers to correct,' Maura explained, directing her cool glance at Clayton. 'I'll call in again some time.'

She left without waiting for a reply, and she drove back to New Ansbach with her throat so tight with tears that it was an agony to swallow. She cursed herself silently. If she could not learn to control herself better in future, then she would have to stay away from Clayton.

Maura's visits to the hospital became less frequent, and they seldom lasted longer than a few minutes. Valerie Austen was there beside his bed whenever Maura arrived, and she was still there when Maura left. It was an agony to see them together, but it was an agony which Maura knew she would have to become accustomed to if Clayton was going to marry the woman.

Clayton had been in hospital for ten days when Maura paid him a visit the Wednesday afternoon, and she was once again an awkward third with Valerie Austen in the only available chair beside his bed.

'I'm told that I may be able to go home on Friday,' Clayton announced shortly after Maura's arrival.

'Oh, but that's wonderful news, darling!' Valerie exclaimed, glancing up at Maura who stood rigidly on the other side of the high hospital bed. 'Don't you agree with me, Maura?'

'Yes . . . wonderful,' Maura echoed dully, using pressure of work as an excuse once again to terminate her visit, but Clayton stopped her before she could reach the door.

'Will I see you at Hilltop House this weekend, Maura?'

'I'm . . . not sure,' she answered him vaguely, that familiar tightness clutching at her throat. 'Perhaps,' she added, walking out of his ward before she allowed him to see those ridiculous tears which she had been unable to suppress.

Maura drove back to New Ansbach as if the devil himself was racing up behind her, and on this occasion she ignored the groaning protestations that came from the engine of her battered Volkswagen. She was feeling miserable and angry, and she was in a wild and desperate mood.

Joan took one look at Maura when she arrived at the cottage, and she frowned with concern. 'Was that Valerie person there again today?'

'Yes!' Maura snapped, but she shook her head ruefully the next instant. 'I'm sorry, Joan. I'm in a filthy mood, and I have no right to take it out on you.'

'I know how you must feel, and you don't have to apologise,' Joan assured her gravely. 'Do you honestly think that Clayton is serious about her?'

'Well, they hold hands, and it's *darling* this, and *darling* that! *Oh, God!*' Maura sat down heavily on one of the lounge chairs and buried her quivering face in her hands to force back those futile tears. 'I don't know why I torment myself like this,' she whispered when she had regained some measure of control.

'I'm going to spend the weekend in Durban with Will,' Joan changed the subject, seating herself in the chair facing Maura, and grimacing. 'It's about time I met my future mother-in-law, but, to tell the truth, I'm scared silly.'

Maura took a deep, calming breath and managed a shaky smile. 'If she's as nice as Will, then I'm sure you'll like her.'

'What are you going to do this weekend? Will you be going home to Hilltop House?'

'I might,' Maura shrugged listlessly. 'Clayton says that he might be discharged from the hospital on Friday.'

'And you're not sure that you want to be there to welcome him home if that Valerie person is going to be there to fawn all over him.' Joan added, her glance questioning, 'Am I right?'

'I'm not sure that I want to be there with or without that Valerie person, as you call her.'

Joan reached across to give Maura a reassuring pat on the arm. 'They say the best cure for any problem is to face it head on.'

'Thanks, I'll remember that.'

Maura smiled wryly. During the past months she had

been like the proverbial donkey bashing its head against the same brick wall, and she could not see how Joan's advice was going to help her.

She did eventually decide to go home that weekend, but only because Angela had made it difficult for her to refuse when she had telephoned to let Maura know that Clayton would definitely be discharged from hospital on the Friday afternoon. Maura had had no desire to be at Hilltop House when Clayton arrived home on Friday, and she had put her name down on the roster to make herself available for duty at the school fête on the Friday evening. She had spent the Saturday morning shopping in town, and it was lunchtime before she arrived at Hilltop House.

Clayton still needed to rest and take things easy, but he had recovered remarkably well from the accident which could so easily have been fatal. His hair had been cropped shorter than usual to make the shaven patch behind his ear look less obvious, but the two weeks in hospital had not robbed him of his healthy tan. There was, however, something different about him. He was quiet; almost too quiet. He was brooding about something, and Maura's apprehension escalated. It was a familiar feeling. She had felt this way at the beginning of the year when she had had to face Clayton with the news that she was going to teach. It was as if that loaded gun was once again being pointed directly at her head, but this time she could not understand why. What had she done? Or what had she *not* done? Was she the cause of it, or was Clayton's brooding mood merely one of the after-effects of the accident?

Clayton murmured something about being tired and he went up to his room directly after dinner the Saturday evening. Maura lingered downstairs in the living-room with Angela until after nine that evening, but she felt uneasy and tense, and she was finally driven to ask,

'Why is Clayton in such a brooding mood?'

'I wish I knew,' Angela sighed, her expression troubled as she put away the tapestry she had been working on. 'He's been in this sombre mood since he arrived home yesterday, but I have no idea what could be the cause of it.'

'I've had a horrible feeling all evening that a storm is about to erupt, and I don't think I want to hang around much longer to discover the reason for it.' A coldness raced up Maura's spine, and she shivered. 'I'm going up to my room.'

'Yes, I think I'm going to have an early night as well,' Angela smiled, rising and accompanying Maura upstairs.

They switched off the lights as they went, and Maura had an uneasy feeling that Clayton's dark, brooding eyes could be observing her from the shadows. It was ridiculous to be so on edge, but for some obscure reason she knew she would not feel safe until she reached the privacy of her bedroom.

Angela paused outside Maura's door and kissed her on the cheek. 'Goodnight, my child,'

'Goodnight, Mother,' Maura responded in a nervous whisper, and she stood watching her stepmother until she entered the bedroom at the end of the long passage. Only then did Maura enter her own room and close the door behind her.

She stood for a long time under the shower while the warm water pummelled her body, and she felt calmer some minutes later when she put on her towelling robe and shook her hair free of her shower cap. She brushed her teeth and pulled a face at herself in the mirror for being such an idiot as to allow Clayton's mood to affect her, and she could almost laugh at herself when she left the bathroom and seated herself on the stool in front of her dressing-table.

She brushed her hair with long easy strokes until it shone like gold in the light above the mirror, and she was reaching for her jar of night cream when she heard her bedroom door being opened quietly. She turned on the stool thinking it was her stepmother, but it was not Angela, and Maura's nerve ends quivered in something close to fear.

Clayton was still fully dressed in his blue open-necked shirt and grey slacks, and she did not like the look on his lean face when he closed the door behind him and walked towards her. His dark, brooding glance flicked over her when she rose nervously from the stool, and she felt a stab of alarm. She was not wearing anything under her towelling robe, and she had an awful suspicion that Clayton was aware of this when his eyes followed the action of her hands as she drew the belt of her robe more firmly about her waist.

Stay calm! she warned herself when her heart started pounding out a frightened tattoo against her ribs. *For God's sake, stay calm!*

'I thought you had gone to bed ages ago,' she said, praising herself silently on the steadiness of her voice when her insides were quaking.

'I went to my room, but I didn't go to bed.' He looked outwardly calm, but Maura sensed a leashed violence in his muscular frame when he walked past her to lower himself on to the window-seat beneath the open window. 'I'm tired of lying down, and I needed to do some thinking.'

'You shouldn't try to do too much too soon,' she warned, hiding her nervous tension behind an equally calm exterior.

'Don't lecture me.' His hawk-like features were strangely taut, and his eyes glittered ominously in the dimly lit room. 'There is an important matter I have to discuss with you.'

'Couldn't it have waited until the morning?'

'It could, but I would prefer to have it out here and now.' His compelling glance held hers relentlessly. 'Why have you been avoiding me, Maura?'

'I haven't been avoiding you,' she denied with a guilty start.

'Haven't you?' he smiled derisively. 'Then may I know why you never came home one weekend during these past two months? And, while you're about it, you might also explain why your visits dropped down to the barest minimum during my stay in hospital?'

Maura gave her belt an extra tug for firmness and pushed her trembling hands into the wide pockets. 'I've been involved in the activities at the school during this past term, and these past weeks have been hectic for the children as well as the teachers.'

'Ah, yes, the children were writing their exams.' He seemed to mock her. 'I suppose I should say that it's nice to have you here at Hilltop House for a weekend after such a long absence, but it's such a pity that I almost had to get myself killed before you would consider to honour us with your presence.'

His scathing remark caught her on the raw. She did not think she would ever forget those agonising hours when, at first, they had not known whether he would live or die and, later, whether he would walk again or spend the rest of his life in a wheelchair. Remembered fear clutched at her chest and her throat, and she clenched her jaw so tightly that it ached.

'That isn't funny!' she hissed through her teeth, turning from him for fear that he might read more into her expression than she wanted him to see.

'I wasn't trying to be funny, but I have something else

to tell you which you might find quite amusing,' he continued derisively. 'I had a dream when I was in hospital. I dreamed that you were sitting next to my bed. You were holding my hand and you were crying. I know you were crying because, in my dream, I could feel the wetness of your tears against my hand, and you were saying something quite incredible.'

Maura felt her heart stop and then race on at a suffocating pace. He knew! He had heard her rambling confession at his bedside! A wave of stinging heat surged into her face when the shock of her discovery subsided, and her embarrassment was so acute that it rendered her immobile and temporarily speechless.

'Do you want to know what you said to me in my dream?' Clayton persisted with a ruthlessness she could not understand. Would it provide him with some savage delight to humiliate her?

'I imagine you're going to tell me whether I want to know or not,' she finally said, and her hands were clenched so tightly in the pockets of her robe that her nails bit painfully into her soft palms.

'The dream was so clear, and I've gone over it so many times in my mind that I can almost quote the words verbatim. You said: "Don't be angry with me, Clayton. I didn't want to fall in love with you, and I tried not to, but I couldn't help it. I guess I've always loved you, and I know I always will".'

Maura had paled at the sound of Clayton's deep, gravelly voice repeating in a mocking undertone the words which had been torn from the depths of her soul, and it felt as if the air was being driven from her lungs when, out of the corner of her eye, she saw him rise from the window-seat.

'Don't you find my dream amusing?' he demanded, coming up behind her, and her nerves leapt in alarm at his nearness.

'No,' she croaked, sensing an element of danger which had intruded into the already strained atmosphere between them. 'No, I don't find it amusing.'

'Why not?'

Why not? Dear God, she loved him so much that she would walk through the fires of hell for him if he asked her to. She loved him so much that being near him was as much a torment as being away from him. Loving him had not only stripped her of her peace of mind, it was gnawing away at her sanity, and there was nowhere she could go to seek refuge from that savage and relentless pain of knowing that he could never love her in return. Did he honestly expect her to find that amusing?

'Look at me, Maura, and answer my question!' His touch was a punishment she did not deserve, and there was an unfathomable anger in his eyes when he spun her round to face him. 'Why don't you find my little tale amusing?'

'For God's sake, Clayton!' Her voice was choked with pain and despair. 'What do you want from me?'

'I want you to tell me that the words that dragged me back to consciousness were not part of a dream.'

She was jolted mentally and physically as if she had been wired to an electrical circuit. What was he trying to do to her? Did he want to bring her humiliatingly to her knees for daring to love him?

They say the best cure for any problem is to face it head on. Joan's advice leapt unbidden into Maura's mind and, strangely, it gave her the strength to do what Clayton expected of her.

'It wasn't a dream,' she said, a deadly calm taking possession of her as she raised her pale face to his with a proud, almost defiant tilt of her chin. 'Everything I said was true. I love you, and I will always love you, but I would never have embarrassed you with my confession if I had known that you were regaining consciousness, and I'd be grateful if you would put it right out of your mind.'

'I have no intention of putting it out of my mind.'

'You don't have to worry, Clayton.' Her mouth quivered uncontrollably, and she turned from him hastily to hide the sheen of tears in her pain-filled eyes. 'I'll get over it without a brotherly lecture from you.'

'Running away isn't going to help, Maura,' he mocked her when she had walked a few paces away to place a comfortable distance between them, and anger came to her rescue as nothing else could have done.

'Tell yourself that!' she snapped, and the atmosphere in her bedroom was suddenly electrified.

'What's that supposed to mean?'

'I'm not running, Clayton,' she said coldly, turning to face him. '*You* are.'

'Dammit, Maura! If I've been running then it has been for your sake, not mine!' he exploded savagely, lessening the distance between them in two long strides to place her at a disadvantage with the height and breadth of him. 'Do you know what it can do to a man of twenty-seven to discover that he has fallen in love with a seventeen-year-old girl whom he has always thought of as a sister? Can you imagine the immense feeling of guilt and self-disgust when he finds that he suddenly can't come near her without being aware of a powerful desire to touch her and make passionate love to her?' Clayton's hands shot out to grip her shoulders, his fingers biting into her soft flesh through her towelling robe, and she bit back a cry of pain as he pulled her roughly against his hard body. 'My God, Maura!' he said thickly, his eyes like smouldering embers in his tortured face, and her heart was suddenly racing so fast that she could scarcely breathe when his hands slid down her back to grind her hips into his. 'You've put me through hell since the night of your seventeenth birthday party when you came down into the hall to welcome your guests. You were no longer a child, you were a sensual and unawakened young woman, and I was insanely jealous of every young man who danced with you that night.'

'Are you aware of what you're saying?' she whispered, her mind reeling in confusion and bewilderment as she placed her hands defensively against his broad chest and leaned away from him.

'Do you know why we fought so much during those years after your seventeenth birthday?' he counter-questioned harshly as if she had not spoken. 'Picking a fight with you was the only way I could protect myself against my desire for you, and I dared not let you get too close. When you spoke about going to college a part of me rejoiced at the knowledge that I would feel safer with temptation out of the way, but a greater part of me selfishly and jealously wanted you here where I could keep an eye on you every day.'

'I don't understand.' She shook her head, her corn-gold hair dancing about her face and shoulders as she stared up at him in wide-eyed disbelief. 'There were times during these past months when I made my feelings disgustingly obvious, but every time you rejected me. Why? If you care about me as you say you do, then why did you do that to me?'

'I'm ten years older than you. I know my own feelings, but I had to be sure about you, and I am now.' His hands trailed over her body and a curious light entered his eyes. 'Are you wearing anything under this robe?'

'No,' she croaked, her cheeks growing warm beneath his fiery gaze, and her pulses rioted out of control when his fingers trailed a tantalising path along her throat down to the vee of her robe, but she could not let him touch her intimately until she knew exactly where she stood. 'Where does Valerie Austen fit into this?' she asked him, twisting herself free and putting a safe distance between them.

'Nowhere!' he answered abruptly, the probing intensity of his eyes not giving her a moment's peace. 'Val is a friend, and someone whom I used shamelessly in my attempts to rid myself of my feelings for you, but she has remained a friend despite the fact that she knows how I feel about you.'

'She knows?' Maura gasped incredulously, and Clayton nodded curtly.

'I telephoned her from Durban and asked her to be here at Hilltop House when we arrived home that day,' he explained, his dark brows drawing together in a frown. 'I wanted to test your reaction, and I think she played her part very well, but you clammed up so tightly that the entire exercise was a failure.'

'Until I poured my heart out to you when I thought you were still unconscious,' she added, her voice choked with emotion.

Relief and happiness blended with an intensity that brought tears to her eyes, and a strangled sob passed her lips as she flung herself into Clayton's arms to bury her face against his chest.

They clung to each other in silence, their mind and their bodies strained closer until Clayton muttered an impatient oath, and tipped her face up to his with gentle fingers to set his mouth on hers.

The barriers were down at last, and they kissed hungrily with a passion long denied. Maura could not think coherently, but she did not want to think at that moment as Clayton urged her towards the bed and lowered her on to it. She simply wanted to enjoy the joyous freedom of expressing her love in a way more explicit than words, and she locked her arms about his neck as she welcomed the weight of his body on hers.

'Your skin smells of gardenias,' he groaned, his mouth leaving hers to explore the sensitive cord of her throat while his fingers gently parted her robe to stroke her breasts, and the pleasure of his touch was so intense that she gasped as the tremors of desire shook through her.

She took his face between her hands and unashamedly guided his hot, seeking mouth down to her breast, and a shaft of aching desire surged into her loins. Clayton moved against her, making her aware of his own fierce need, and her hips arched involuntarily towards his, seeking to be closer still to this man she loved so deeply, but Clayton leashed his emotions with admirable control. His eyes were so dark they were almost black with the extent of his feelings when he eased himself away from her and pushed himself up on to his elbow.

'You know me with all my faults, Kitten,' he murmured in a throaty, unfamiliar voice, his fingers probing and caressing her nipples until they were throbbing with desire, and she almost cried out in protest when he ceased his erotic manipulations to pull the front of her robe across her naked breasts. 'Do you think you could bear spending the rest of your life with me as your husband and your lover?'

'Oh, Clayton, I have faults too,' she whispered unsteadily, her eyes misty in her flushed face as she traced a loving finger along the strong line of his jaw. 'You've had to put up with all my faults almost from the moment of my birth, but do you think you could cope with them for the rest of your life?'

'I think neither of us really has a choice,' he said gravely, his voice vibrant with emotion as he combed his fingers through the long, silky hair splayed out about her head. 'I love you, Maura.'

'I love you too,' she murmured huskily, allowing him to see into her heart as he was allowing her to see into his. 'I love you so very, *very* much.'

She drew his head down to hers, her lips parting beneath his to welcome the intimate invasion of his tongue, and she trembled with the force of the emotions clamouring through her. Her fingers tugged impatiently at the buttons of his shirt, and she slipped her hands inside to explore his warm, hair-roughened chest, the soft pads of her fingers delighting in the firm texture of his skin.

'I like what you're doing, Maura, but you're playing with fire,' he groaned, easing his mouth from hers and making her squeal when he nipped her earlobe between his teeth. 'I may not be a hundred per cent fit yet, but I'm not sexually incapacitated, and I happen to want you so badly that I'll need very little encouragement to do what ought to wait until after we're married.'

A wave of heat surged into her cheeks, and she avoided the teasing light in his eyes as she pushed him away from her to get up off the bed. She crossed the room to lower herself on to the window-seat, and she drew the cool night air deeply into her lungs to ease the tension of desire in her body.

'Talking about marriage . . .'

'It will have to be the Saturday when the school holidays begin so that we can have a decent honeymoon before you have to return to work,' Clayton filled in when she hesitated to collect her thoughts, and she turned her head sharply to find him on the window-seat beside her.

'You're not serious.'

'I most certainly am.' He smiled into her incredulous grey eyes. 'I've waited long enough for you to grow up,

Kitten, and I'm not going to prolong the wait a day longer than I have to.'

'I suppose you do realise that you're giving me no more than six days to make the necessary preparations?' she demanded, her eyes sparkling with humour despite her attempt at a stern expression.

'Mother will help.'

Yes, Mother would help, she thought, a tremulous smile curving her soft mouth when she tried to imagine Angela's reaction to their news, and she could not even begin to guess at Joan's reaction when she told her that she was going to marry Clayton.

'Oh, Clayton!' she sighed, her pulse-rate quickening at the look in his eyes which she knew, at last, was meant only for her, and she altered her position on the window-seat so that she could lie curled up in his arms. 'I doubt if I shall sleep tonight.'

'I know I shan't,' he laughed softly into her fragrant hair. 'I shall be thinking of you all night. I shall be thinking of holding you like this, and the nights when I shan't have to kiss you goodnight and leave you.'

Maura turned her head slightly and pressed her warm, quivering lips to his bare chest. She could hear his heart beating as heavily as her own, and then a familiar sound warbled into the room.

'The nightjar is back.' She smiled into his broad chest, a deep sense of peace and contentment enveloping her. 'I'm so glad he made it.'

'I wonder if his passage was as difficult as ours,' Clayton murmured with a smile in his voice as he got up, drawing Maura to her feet and into his arms. 'I would like to hold you like this all night, but the desire to touch you and make love to you is a delightful torment which I'm finding difficult to endure.' His arms tightened about her and he kissed her hard and satisfyingly on the lips before he set her aside. 'Goodnight, my darling, and dream of me.'

My darling. A melting warmth swept through her as she wished him goodnight, and her happiness was so intense that it felt as if her heart would burst as she watched him leave her room and close the door softly behind him.

'Clayton . . .' She whispered his name almost reverently some minutes later when she lay in bed, and she smiled and stretched lazily as she felt herself drifting into that hazy world of dreams.

Dreams had a habit of fading in the dawn light, but Maura knew that her most important dream was a reality which would still be there when she awoke in the morning. It was real, it was vital, and it would last for always.

*Exciting, adventurous, sensual stories
of love long ago*

On Sale Now:

SATAN'S ANGEL by Kristin James

*Slater was the law in a land that was as wild and untamed
as he was himself, but all that changed when he met
Victoria Stafford. She had been raised to be a lady, but
that didn't mean she had no will of her own. Their search
for her kidnapped cousin brought them together, but they
were too much alike for the course of true love to run
smooth.*

PRIVATE TREATY by Kathleen Eagle

*When Jacob Black Hawk rescued schoolteacher
Carolina Hammond from a furious thunderstorm, he
swept her off her feet in every sense of the word, and she
knew that he was the only man who would ever make her
feel that way. But society had put barriers between them
that only the most powerful and overwhelming love could
overcome . . .*

Look for them wherever Harlequin books are sold.

Temptation™

TEMPTATION WILL BE
EVEN HARDER TO RESIST...

In September, Temptation is presenting a sophisticated new face to the world. A fresh look that truly brings Harlequin's most intimate romances into focus.

What's more, all-time favorite authors Barbara Delinsky, Rita Clay Estrada, Jayne Ann Krentz and Vicki Lewis Thompson will join forces to help us celebrate. The result? A very special quartet of Temptations...

- **Four striking covers**
- **Four stellar authors**
- **Four sensual love stories**
- **Four variations on one spellbinding theme**

All in one great month! Give in to Temptation in September.

Can you keep a secret?

You can keep this one plus 4 free novels